"Jared, please let me go. If you won't help me, I'll have to look elsewhere for what I need," Tabor said.

"What you need?" he asked, his voice a low rumble. "Just what is it that you need, Miss O'Casey? Need. That's a fascinating word. I *need* to kiss you. I *need* to feel your hair sliding through my hands as I hold you close, very close. Do you understand what I'm asking?"

Oh, yes, Tabor thought dreamily. Then she realized what she'd said. "No!" She pressed her hands flat on his chest and pushed. She could feel the hard muscles beneath her palms, and knew her efforts to shove Jared away were futile. "I don't want—"

"Don't you?" he asked. He grasped her arms, hauled her to her feet, and kissed her, his mouth hard against hers.

Need. Fierce, undeniable, irresistible . . .

WHAT ARE *LOVESWEPT* ROMANCES?

They are stories of true romance and touching emotion. We believe those two very important ingredients are constants in our highly sensual and very believable stories in the *LOVESWEPT* line. Our goal is to give you, the reader, stories of consistently high quality that may sometimes make you laugh, sometimes make you cry, but are always fresh and creative and contain many delightful surprises within their pages.

Most romance fans read an enormous number of books. Those they truly love, they keep. Others may be traded with friends and soon forgotten. We hope that each *LOVESWEPT* romance will be a treasure—a "keeper." We will always try to publish

LOVE STORIES YOU'LL NEVER FORGET
BY AUTHORS YOU'LL ALWAYS REMEMBER

The Editors

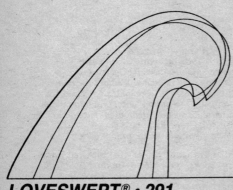

LOVESWEPT® • 291

Joan Elliott Pickart
Man of the Night

BANTAM BOOKS
TORONTO • NEW YORK • LONDON • SYDNEY • AUCKLAND

MAN OF THE NIGHT
A Bantam Book / November 1988

LOVESWEPT® and the wave device are registered trade-
marks of Bantam Books, a division of Bantam Doubleday
Dell Publishing Group, Inc. Registered in U.S. Patent and
Trademark Office and elsewhere.

If you would be interested in receiving protective vinyl
covers for your Loveswept books, please write to this address
for information:

Loveswept
Bantam Books
P.O. Box 985
Hicksville, NY 11802

ISBN 0-553-21943-X

Published simultaneously in the United States and Canada

Bantam Books are published by Bantam Books, a division
of Bantam Doubleday Dell Publishing Group, Inc. Its trademark, consisting of the words "Bantam Books" and the
portrayal of a rooster, is Registered in U.S. Patent and
Trademark Office and in other countries. Marca Registrada.
Bantam Books, 666 Fifth Avenue, New York, New York
10103.

PRINTED IN THE UNITED STATES OF AMERICA

O   0 9 8 7 6 5 4 3 2 1

One

The Miracles Casino in Las Vegas, Nevada, was the epitome of glamour and glitz. To step within its doors was to be transported into a world just beyond reality. Thick burgundy-colored carpet stretched in all directions and a multitude of chandeliers hung from the ceiling, burning brightly twenty-four hours a day. At the many velvet-covered tables the male card dealers wore black tuxedoes; the women were in long black gowns. Cocktail waitresses clad in thigh-length velvet outfits of black and burgundy and black fishnet stockings circled constantly through the rooms. In one corridor slot machines gleamed as they stood in rows like soldiers at attention, waiting to be commanded into action.

To enter Miracles was to be wrapped in an aura of opulence, to have the strange sensation that one deserved to be there. Excitement hummed constantly in the air, and that intangible quality of anticipation about what would come with the next roll of the dice, spin of the roulette wheel, pull of the arm on the slot machine.

Miracles lived up to its name.

Jared Loring stood at the top of a curved, sweeping staircase and surveyed the bustle of activity below. His gaze swept over the clusters of people in the huge expanse, missing no detail. He could see instantly any sign of trouble, sense any subtle hint that things were not exactly as they should be. He moved slowly down the stairs, still looking, satisfying himself that all was well.

The staircase had been Jared's indulgence to himself. To him it was an elegant touch of the South, a reminder of the era of Southern plantations when men were true gentlemen, protecting the honor of ladies who had perfected the art of speaking with their eyes above coyly fluttering fans.

The stairs led to the private office and suites above the gaming floor, and a velvet rope at their foot kept patrons of the casino from going up. But they could look, and could mentally transport themselves back to the days of Scarlett and Rhett, and romance.

Jared unhooked the velvet rope and stepped around it, then put it back in place. Again he scanned the area, ignoring the appreciative glances he received from many women. The casino was especially busy that night, summer having brought in tourists from all parts of the country, even the world, but the noise level was controlled by carefully constructed acoustics.

Jared's perusal told him that everything was fine. Everything except himself.

A cocktail waitress strolled past him, adding an extra sway to her hips. " 'Evening, Mr. Loring."

"Hello, Ellen," he said, nodding absently. There was a faint Southern accent in his deep voice.

Another waitress walked toward him from the opposite direction. "Hello, Mr. Loring," she said, her gaze sliding over his perfectly tailored tuxedo.

"Hello, Beth," he said. He hardly looked at her, watching instead as his second-in-command, Nick Capoletti, wove his way through the crowds to him. Dressed in an expensive tuxedo, Nick was, Jared saw, receiving a great deal of female scrutiny and approval. With his impressive build and dark Italian good looks, Nick never went unnoticed.

"You're down early . . . again," Nick said when he reached Jared. "And you're scowling . . . again. You look more like a mean, lean bouncer than the owner of this place."

"Half owner," Jared said, his frown deepening. "Let us not forget my notorious partner, Tucker Boone."

Nick chuckled and shook his head. "Jared, you've been so tense the past week, you're like a racehorse in the gate. I'm going to say this one more time. Tucker is about to become a father. I can't believe he's giving any thought to that bet he made with you a year ago."

"Ha! And it's one year minus two weeks. I have two weeks to go before I win this one. Tuck is sneaky, Nick. He's up to something, I just know he is."

"You guys are crazy," Nick said, laughing. "He bet you a thousand dollars a year ago that you'd fall in love within the next year. What are you so strung out about? You have only two weeks left, and I know there's no one special in your life. You need a score card to keep up with all the women you see. From where I'm standing, you've got nothing to worry about."

"Ha!" Jared said again. "You don't know Tucker Boone as well as I do. Alison and the baby or not, Tuck is thinking about our bet, you can make book on it. There's a lot at stake here, Capoletti."

"A thousand dollars?" Nick raised his eyebrows. "Come on, Jared, that's loose change for you."

"No, the money isn't important. It's the bet itself, the fact that if I lose, it means I've fallen in love." He shook his head. "Oh, Lord, spare me. I saw Tucker when he first fell in love with Alison. He couldn't string two sentences together without getting a foolish grin on his face. No way, not me. I control every aspect of my life, I'm in charge. Love can have a guy running in circles. It can also knock a man over before he knows what has hit him. I'm telling you, Nick, I'm staying on my guard for the next two weeks."

Nick shrugged. "So don't see any women."

"A monk I'm not, Capoletti," Jared said, glowering at him. "I just have to watch out for new faces, a woman Tucker could have decided was perfect for me and then figured out a way to wiggle her into my life."

"Sounds like you're staying on top of the situation. Why are you so uptight about it?"

Jared sighed. "There's something you don't know."

"Oh?"

"Tuck and I have had hundreds of bets over the years, all kinds of stuff."

"And?"

"Nick," Jared said gloomily, "I've lost every one. I'm lucky in casinos, at the track, you name it. But in a bet with Tucker Boone? Something always goes wrong. I lose."

Nick's eyes widened. "Every one?"

Jared nodded, looking more miserable by the moment.

Nick whistled low and long. "Amazing. No wonder you're a wreck."

"Tell me about it. The next two weeks could very well be the longest of my thirty-six years on this earth."

"Lost every bet with Tucker Boone," Nick said, wandering away. "Amazing."

Jared scowled as Nick disappeared into a throng of people. So Tucker had uncanny good luck, he thought sullenly. That was all. But not this time, by damn. This was one bet Jared Loring had no intention of losing. Two more weeks and he'd be home free. Two long, teeth-grinding, tension-packed weeks. Hell.

For the next half hour Jared strolled through the casino, stopping to speak with the many people who greeted him. Nick had been right. Jared was on the floor early. He'd fallen into that habit lately as he'd become more restless and edgy, unable to sit still in his large, comfortably furnished suite upstairs.

Nick would go off duty soon, and Jared would take over for the night. He preferred the night, and the people it brought to Miracles. Along with the tourists would be the high rollers, the serious gamblers, the jet-setters. Jared could spot the real ones from the phonies a room away, and knew many of his rich, powerful, and wealthy patrons on a first-name basis.

He knew their secrets too. He knew which smiles

were forced to cover inner sadness of empty lives and broken dreams, of happiness sought but never found. He knew who could really afford to lose at the roulette wheel and laugh, and who was there in a last-ditch effort to win what was needed to carry on his or her present life-style. When they left Miracles, he was aware of where they went, what transpired in their lives until they returned to his oasis, who was now financially secure, and who had inched to the edge of desperation.

Oh, yes, Jared liked the night. It hid in its darkness stories he would never tell, alliances many would question in the light of day. The night suited him, for within it he could find whatever he needed: excitement, women, peace, danger. The night wrapped itself around him with a cloak of familiarity, a sense of belonging. It contained a world he understood and accepted.

Jared's reverie was interrupted by a quiet beep that caught no one's attention but his own. He reached inside his jacket and withdrew a flat device no bigger than a pocket comb. There were a dozen quarter-inch grooves on the metal plate, one of which was glowing bright red. The beep sounded again. Jared pressed a small button to silence the mechanism, slid it back into his pocket, and started across the casino. He moved quickly, yet gave the impression that he was in no particular hurry. He smiled, nodded at several people, and arrived at an elevator in a side corridor three seconds before Nick.

"Your suite," Nick said.

"Yes," Jared said, inserting a key in the panel next to the elevator doors.

The two men entered the elevator. The doors

swished closed, and Jared unbuttoned his jacket. Seconds later the elevator bumped to a stop, the doors opened, and Jared and Nick stepped out into a hall carpeted in the same plush burgundy as the casino. Three men in brown uniforms with holstered guns were waiting for them.

"Wait here," Jared said to the men. "Come on, Nick, let's see what's doing."

"You pay those guys a lot of money to handle this stuff," Nick said, matching Jared's long-legged stride down the hall.

"Could be nothing," Jared said.

"Could be something," Nick said.

"We'll see."

Outside the door of his suite, Jared pulled a gun from the back of his belt and waved Nick against the wall on one side of the door. Crouching low, Jared turned the knob, then pushed the door open at the same time he flattened himself against the corridor wall. Silence.

Nick looked at Jared questioningly, Jared shook his head, and they waited. Seconds ticked by.

There was the sound of a rather exasperated sigh, then a woman's voice broke the tense silence.

"Do come in, Mr. Loring," she said. "After all, this is your apartment. I assume you have a gun. I don't. It's quite safe to enter."

Jared raised one hand to indicate that Nick should stay where he was. Nick nodded. Jared spun away from the wall, bent his knees, and held the gun at the ready in both hands in the open doorway.

He was pointing a loaded gun at the most beautiful woman he'd ever seen. In a flash every inch of her was imprinted on his mind. She was tall, maybe five-seven, in her mid-twenties, and was wearing a teal-blue silk and chiffon cocktail dress that molded lovingly her full breasts and tiny waist, and revealed a great deal of shapely legs. She had a lovely delicate face, with large dark brown eyes. Wavy blond hair tumbled to the middle of her back. She was stunning.

Jared slowly straightened and dropped one hand from the gun. He kept the weapon trained on the woman standing in the middle of his living room.

"There's no need for that gun," she said. "I told you that I don't have one. Are you planning on searching me?"

"It's a thought." His gaze slid over her slowly, appreciatively, then he met her eyes again. "A very interesting thought."

"Would anyone mind," Nick asked, "if I unglued myself from this wall?"

"Come on in, Nick," Jared said, "and meet our visitor."

Nick stood behind Jared, who had not gone farther into the room. He glanced at the woman, at the gun Jared still pointed at her, then back at the woman.

"Keep her company while I look around," Jared said.

Nick shrugged and entered as Jared crossed the living room to the bedroom beyond. Nick closed the door, leaned against it, and folded his arms loosely over his chest.

"Read any good books lately?" he asked the woman pleasantly. "By the way, I'm Nick Capoletti."

The woman just looked at him, her face expressionless.

He smiled. "You've been rendered speechless by

my incredible body, my fabulous good looks, and my overwhelming charm, right?"

"All clear," Jared said, coming back into the living room. "You can go, Nick. I'll handle this. Tell the security men that everything is under control."

"I could stay," Nick said.

Jared walked to the door. "No, it's not necessary."

"Who is she?" Nick whispered. "How did she get this far without setting off alarms? Have you ever seen her before?"

"No," Jared said, his voice also hushed, "but there's no doubt in my mind as to how she knew how to get past the security systems and why she's here."

"Oh?"

Jared narrowed his eyes. "Tucker Boone."

"Ah." Nick nodded. "The light dawns. Clever, very clever. I must say, Jared, Tucker has good taste."

"True, but it isn't going to work. I'm one step ahead of Mr. Boone."

Nick opened the door. "Well, enjoy," he said cheerfully. "Nice meeting you, ma'am," he added over his shoulder.

Jared closed the door, slipped his gun back into his belt, and turned to face the woman. She really was beautiful, he thought. Her hair was sensational, calling to him to sink his hands into it, to sift it through his fingers like golden, silken threads. It would float over her body, over his. Naked bodies. Bodies eager and willing to make love.

He cleared his throat as heat gathered low and heavy within him. "Your name?" he asked gruffly.

"Tabor," she said.

And he was Jared Loring, she thought. She'd heard about him for years from her father, but as prepared as she had thought she was to meet Jared in person at last, she was definitely not prepared. He had been a name that went along with the stories her father told, a man she felt she had known forever. What her father hadn't told her was that Jared Loring was incredibly handsome. His attractively rugged face was tanned, his unusual silver hair thick and shiny. He had the bluest eyes she'd ever seen, and his custom-tailored tuxedo fit exquisitely over his tightly muscled physique. No, she had not been prepared for the raw sensuality that emanated from this man, the unspoken power and virility. There was an aura about him of seething energy that could erupt at any moment or be tamped down at his will. Jared Loring was a very dangerous man, she mused.

"Tabor," he repeated. "Something Tabor? Or Tabor Something?"

She lifted her chin. "My name is Tabor O'Casey."

A flicker of surprise crossed his face, then his expression was bland again. "O'Casey."

"That's correct. You knew my father, Cat O'Casey. He died a month ago of a heart attack."

This wasn't adding up, Jared thought. How in the hell had Tucker found out about his involvement with Cat O'Casey? Cat had been a man of the night, no one Tucker had ever met or knew anything about. Could Tucker have paid off the right people to gain the information that would enable him to plant this gorgeous creature in Jared's lap with a plausible story? Nice move, Boone. Very sharp.

"I heard that Cat passed away," Jared said. "My sympathies. Why don't we sit down? Would you like a drink?"

"No, thank you." Tabor settled into a dark blue easy chair and crossed her legs.

Jared walked over to the bar against the far wall, poured himself a Scotch, then sat down in a matching chair opposite Tabor. He lifted his glass.

"To Tucker Boone," he said dryly. "Nice try, but no cigar. I have to give him credit though. You're an extremely beautiful woman . . . Tabor."

"Thank you, but I'm afraid I don't know anyone named Tucker Boone." She paused. "Mr. Loring—"

"Call me Jared. We're just one big happy family here. I'll call you Tabor until you decide to tell me what your real name is." He took a swallow of liquor. "You're really very good, you know. If I didn't know better, I'd say from the expression on your face that you're actually confused and have no idea what I'm talking about. But you and I are very aware of what I'm talking about. You're welcome to call Tucker, if you wish, and tell him it didn't work. Then, because I'm such a good sport, I'll buy you dinner. I suppose I'll have to change some of the security system now that you know it. Tell Tucker the bill is all his. Just how much information did he give you on the system?"

Tabor sighed. Wonderful, she thought. All through the years while her father had been telling her enthralling stories of the daring deeds of Jared Loring, Cat had failed to mention that the gorgeous Mr. Loring was a fruitcake. After blithering on about someone named Tucker Boone, insinuating that her name wasn't Tabor O'Casey and she was playing a role of some kind, he calmly announced he'd buy her dinner! Jared was a cuckoo, and she'd been hoping he'd help her.

"Don't look so upset," he said. "You win some, you lose some. I imagine Tucker paid you well to get this far. Come on, give. What did he tell you about the security system? I need to get it changed right away. I could ask him, I suppose."

"Would you stop it?" Tabor exclaimed in a loud voice. Jared frowned, obviously surprised at her outburst. "I don't know anyone named Tucker Boone," she continued. "I came up in the service elevator, which was standing open in the kitchen. I picked your lock. Difficult, yes. Impossible, no. I wasn't able to find the control panel near the door to turn off the rest of your equipment, so I moved under the sensors in that phony mirror on the wall. I was tripped up, I'd guess, by body-heat detectors. Very sophisticated, Mr. Loring, but then, according to everything my father told me about you over the years, I expected it to be. My purpose was to speak with you without anyone knowing I was here." She stood up. "This is obviously a waste of time, and time is something I can't spare."

"Sit down."

"I'm sorry for any inconvenience that I—"

"Sit . . . down."

Tabor sat. There was no way on earth, she decided, that anyone with even half a brain would ignore the steely edge of command in Jared's voice. A person would have to be as crazy as he not to do as instructed when Jared made up his mind about how it was to be. Oh, yes, he was a very, very dangerous man.

Damn, what was going on here, Jared wondered. He'd seen a flicker of vulnerability in Tabor's eyes, a hint of desperation. Was it possible that she was actually Cat O'Casey's daughter? An O'Casey could have gotten this far past the security system.

No, he thought. Tucker had sent her. Tuck had done his homework, bought some information, and sent this delectable creature to him. And, no doubt about it, she was an excellent choice. She was just so damn beautiful! The heat throbbing low in his body was evidence enough that he was acutely aware of the feminine attributes of the supposed Miss Tabor O'Casey.

But it was more than that, Jared realized. Something about this woman was urging him to go to her, to hold her, to tell her that whatever had caused that glimpse of pain in her eyes, he'd take care of it. He wanted to soothe her fears, keep her from harm. And he wanted to make love to her. He wanted to touch her and feel her come alive with passion beneath him, wrap himself in her softness and scent and tangle his hands in the glorious cascade of her incredible hair.

"Damn," he muttered, shifting in his chair as his body reacted to his thoughts. "Look, this isn't getting us anywhere. Why don't you just admit that Tucker sent you, and that will be that."

Tabor threw up her hands. "Fine. Tucker sent me. May I go now?"

Jared narrowed his eyes, draining his glass before setting it on an end table. He crossed his arms over his chest and stared at Tabor. She met his gaze. Again silent seconds ticked by. When Jared abruptly smacked the arm of the chair with his hand, Tabor jumped.

"This just doesn't feel right," he said, shaking his head. "It should be open and shut. Tucker Boone is behind this, and I caught him. Yet . . ." He stood, pushed his jacket back, and planted his hands on his hips. "A little voice in my head is whispering that maybe there's more to this than meets the eye. That voice has kept me alive on several occasions, and I pay attention to it. Until I'm sure about what's happening here, you're not going to move."

"I don't have time to play games with you," Tabor said, her voice rising. "You're a nut case. You even hear voices."

She really wished he wouldn't stand there like that, looking so darn male. His shirt was stretched tightly across his broad chest, and his pants were molded to his hard thighs. And that hair. Why hadn't her father ever mentioned that Jared's hair was silver before its time, rich and thick and shiny. No, her father wouldn't think about it, nor would he mention the fact that Jared's eyes were as blue as a summer sky. She definitely had not been prepared for all that was Jared Loring.

"Jared, please, let me go. You obviously aren't going to help me, and I'll have to look elsewhere for what I need."

Jared dropped his hands and walked over to her. He gripped the arms of her chair and bent down, pinning her in place as she looked up at him with wide eyes.

"What do you need?" he said, his voice a low rumble. "Just what is it that you need, Miss O'Casey? Need. That's a fascinating word. I *need* to kiss you. I *need* to feel that hair of yours sliding through my hands as I hold you close, very close, to me. Are we on the same wavelength with our needs?"

Oh, yes, Tabor thought dreamily. Then she blinked.

"No!" She pressed her hands flat on his chest and pushed. She could feel the hard muscles beneath her palms, and was assaulted by the aromas of soap and musky aftershave, and an essence that was pure male. She was very aware that her efforts to shove Jared away were futile. "I don't want—"

"Don't you?" he interrupted.

He grasped her upper arms, hauled her to her feet, and kissed her, his mouth hard against hers.

Sensations exploded within Jared like rockets spinning out of control. He parted Tabor's lips, delved his tongue into her mouth, and drank of a sweetness like none he'd ever known. His hands left her arms to sink into the golden treasure of her hair, which whispered through his fingers like gossamer threads. Heat roared through his body, blood pounded in his veins. The kiss gentled as he drew her to him, nestling the soft curves of her body to the hardness of his own.

Need, his mind echoed. Tabor.

Tabor returned Jared's kiss in total abandon, unable to stop herself, unable to think. She could only feel, glorying in the desire that consumed her. Never before had she experienced a kiss such as this. Her troubles and fears fled into oblivion. Each of her senses seemed sharper as her body hummed with the awareness of her own femininity, and of Jared's masculinity.

Her hands inched upward, her fingers sinking into the silvery depths of Jared's hair. Her breasts were crushed to his chest in a sweet pain, and she craved the soothing touch of his hands to stop the ache. Desire curled deep inside her, growing with each stroke of Jared's tongue as it dueled with hers.

There was nothing beyond this moment, she thought hazily. Nothing beyond the passion burning within her, the need for this man Jared. He was carrying her away so fast to a faraway paradise from which she'd have no wish to return until her hunger for him had been satisfied. She wanted him as she'd wanted no man before, and she would go with him willingly, become one with him, make love with Jared Loring.

Jared tore his mouth from hers to draw a rough breath, then trailed nibbling kisses down her slender neck. He was painfully aroused, aching with the need to bury himself deep within her honeyed warmth and appease his raging hunger for her. His hands dove beneath her hair to her back, sliding down to her buttocks and pressing her against the hard evidence of his desire. He was slipping over the edge of control but didn't care. He had to have, he *would have*, Tabor O'Casey.

"Tabor," he murmured, his Southern accent more pronounced than ever. "Tabor, I want you."

"Yes," she whispered. The sound of her name spoken in that rich drawl was like velvet stroking her. Dear heaven, how she wanted this man. "Oh, yes. Say my name again. It's so beautiful, the way you say my name."

Her name.

The words slammed against Jared's brain like painful blows from a hammer. He knew only what she *claimed* her name to be. And her desire, the surrendering to him, the passionate response to his kiss and touch? Were those, too, part of the role she was playing? Dammit, he'd come too close to forgetting everything but the woman in his arms and his uncontrollable want of her. That had never happened to him before. Not to Jared Loring!

He stiffened and pulled her arms from around his neck. She slowly opened her eyes and met a gaze that was shockingly cold. Jared's eyes were not a smoky blue with desire but were like chips of ice. A muscle jerked in his jaw as he took a step backward and she staggered slightly on her trembling legs.

"Jared?" she asked in confusion.

"That's *my* name," he said, his voice low and harsh. "Why don't we back up all the way to what yours is."

"I . . ."

He spun around and crossed the room to the bar, raking a restless hand through his hair. He splashed more Scotch into a glass, then turned to face her, lifting the glass into the air.

"Here's to you and your performance, ma'am," he said sarcastically.

Performance, he thought. Why did that cause a knot to twist in his gut? Why did it matter that none of what he'd just shared with Tabor was real? Why was it taking every ounce of control he possessed not to carry her to his bed and make love to her through the night, not caring that she wasn't who she claimed to be? What strange spell had this Tabor O'Casey cast over him?

"You're good, very good, at what you do." He tossed off the drink and slammed the glass onto the bar.

Tabor jerked at the loud noise, her eyes widening as the realization of what Jared was saying cut through the last of the mist clouding her mind. She wrapped her arms around her waist and stared at him.

"Performance?" she repeated, her voice not quite

steady. "You think I kissed you like that as part of—of an act, a role I'm playing?"

"Damn right I do, lady. Well, the show is over. Tucker chose well when he picked you. I've never . . ." His jaw tightened even more. "Forget it."

Fury grew within Tabor like a seething volcano, gaining force until it became a scalding wave of anger ready to obliterate Jared Loring. She marched across the room to stand in front of him, glaring up at him.

"How dare you say such despicable things. That kiss was real. Everything I felt, everything I gave, was real. You"—she poked him in the chest, and his eyes widened in surprise—"are a sleazeball. I won't be dragged into the gutter, where your mind operates. I won't be made to feel cheap just because that's all you understand. I am Tabor O'Casey, mister, and as of this moment I don't give a hoot in hell if you believe me or not."

"I—"

"Shut up!" Jared snapped his mouth closed. "I came here, Mr. Loring, because my father told me that if I was ever in trouble I should come to you, and you'd help me. And what do I get? The most glorious kiss I've ever had in my life, and filthy accusations from a man who isn't playing with a full deck. Well, I'm walking out of here right now, and I swear to heaven that if you try to stop me, I'll scream so loud the Marines will show up. I feel sorry for you, Jared Loring. You've spent so many years looking for the evil in people, you don't know the truth when it hits you between the eyes. Or, to be more precise, when it's kissing you with desire so real, so

. . . oh, just go to hell." She whirled around and started toward the door.

Emotions warred within Jared, pulling and pushing him until he felt as though he were being torn in two. For the first time since he could remember, he didn't know what to do, didn't know fact from fiction. The only thing that was clear was that he could not allow this woman to walk out of his life and leave him with an aching body and unanswered questions. He had to know the truth. He didn't know why, but she couldn't leave, not yet.

"Tabor."

Oh, don't, she pleaded silently, her hand on the doorknob. Jared mustn't say her name in that deep velvety voice, gentle now, not harsh or accusing. He mustn't cause the hot desire within her to spread. She had to leave, find someone, somewhere, to help her. She was filled with enough guilt as it was to think she'd placed her attraction to Jared ahead of her reason for seeing him. She had to go. Now.

"Tabor, wait."

"No," she whispered, shaking her head. Her back was to him, her hand still on the doorknob.

Jared crossed the room and placed his hands lightly on her shoulders. He could feel a tremor sweep through her.

"We have to talk," he said quietly. "We . . . I can't leave it like this, not knowing . . ." Lord, listen to him. He was practically begging her to stay. He was so rattled, he'd do well to remember his own name, let alone be able to determine if Tabor was telling the truth about hers. Things like this didn't happen to him. He was a man of control, of razor-sharp reflexes and a sixth sense about people. All of that had served him well in the past, but was useless at that moment. He felt stripped bare and knew only that Tabor mustn't go yet. "Talk to me, Tabor."

"No."

He increased the pressure of his hands, making it clear that he wanted her to face him, but he wouldn't force her. She stiffened, and he knew she was deciding whether to go or stay. His heart thundered in his chest, and he inwardly cursed his own weakness, his driving need to keep her with him.

She turned slowly, looking down at the floor. He dropped his hands to his sides. When she lifted her head to meet his gaze, he stifled a moan. Tears were shimmering in her brown eyes.

"My name is Tabor O'Casey," she said in a trembling voice. "My father was Cat O'Casey, and I loved him so much, but he died, and . . . He told me, always told me, that you would help me if I were in trouble." Tears spilled onto her cheeks. "I'm so frightened. I didn't know what to do, so I came to you just as my father said I should. I don't know anyone named Tucker Boone. The kiss . . . what I felt . . . was real. I'm real, but I can't convince you of that, so I must go to someone else."

Jared cradled her face in his hands and stroked away her tears with his thumbs.

"My name," she said, nearly choking on a sob, "is Tabor O'Casey."

Their gazes held for a timeless moment, then Jared spoke.

"Hello, Tabor O'Casey," he said, his voice strangely hoarse. "I'm Jared Loring, and I'm very, *very* glad you're here."

"Oh, Jared."

He gathered her close to his body, holding her as she clutched the lapels of his jacket in tight fists. She fought back her tears while he simply held her in the safe circle of his arms.

She *was* Tabor O'Casey, he thought. He knew that now with no doubt, though he didn't know why he was so suddenly sure. He was going to quiet her fears, fix whatever it was that was causing her distress. He was going to protect her, keep her from harm. And when the time was right, he'd make love to her, exquisite love, like nothing he'd experienced before.

Because she was Tabor O'Casey . . .

Two

Tabor drew a deep, steadying breath, then slowly, reluctantly, moved out of Jared's arms, away from his strength. She walked to the middle of the room, dashing the last of the tears from her cheeks, then turned to face him.

"I'm sorry," she said. "I'm not a crier. I don't usually fall apart like this. I learned a long time ago to stand on my own two feet and take care of myself. It's just that so much has happened, and I don't know what to do."

"So you came to me," he said, "and I accused you of . . . I'm sorry, Tabor. Look, why don't I have some dinner sent up, then you can tell me what's wrong, right from the top."

"I don't think I could eat anything."

"Give it a try." He crossed the room and picked up the receiver to the phone.

"I'd like to splash some water on my face," she said.

He pointed to the bedroom, then called the kitchen.

Tabor retrieved her purse from a chair and left the living room. After ordering dinner, Jared punched in another number.

"Mrs. Tuttle," a woman answered on the other end of the line.

"Turtle? Jared. Page Nick and have him call me, would you please? I'm in my suite."

"You're in your coffin if you call me Turtle again, General Lee."

Jared chuckled. "You know you love me as though I were your own grandson, Turtle."

"Nick I adore. You? You are a rogue. I'll page my darling Nicky for you."

"You're hurting my feelings, Turtle."

"I'd like to smack your bottom. Good-bye, General Grant."

Jared replaced the receiver, keeping his hand on it as he stared at the open doorway to the bedroom. The telephone rang and he snatched it up.

"It's Nick. I got Turtle's page. What's up?"

"I won't be down for a while," Jared said.

"You're not even due down here for a while, but I'll cover if you're late. Did you solve the problem up there? What did Tucker say when you told him he'd lost this round?"

"My visitor wasn't sent by Tuck." Jared watched Tabor as she came back into the room. "No, Tucker Boone had nothing to do with this." Tabor sat down in the easy chair and met his gaze.

"You're kidding," Nick said.

"What?" Jared asked, forcing himself to look away from Tabor.

"Jared, are you all right?"

"Yeah, sure, I'm fine. I'll be down later."

"Well, call me if you need me."

"Right," Jared said, and hung up. He shrugged out of his jacket and draped it over the back of a chair, then unclipped the holster at the back of his belt and put it on a small table near the door. "Dinner will be up soon." He settled into another easy chair and propped one ankle on the opposite knee. "Talk to me," he said, smiling at Tabor.

"I don't know where to start. You're going to be shocked, I'm afraid, when you learn that Cat O'Casey didn't believe in keeping secrets from his children. We were all he had after my mother died when I was eight."

"We?"

"I have an older brother named Finn. I'm twenty-six, Finn is twenty-nine. We, the three of us, are . . . were very close. After my mother died, Cat told us it was time we knew all about his life, because he'd have to continue to leave us from time to time as he'd always done. Our mother had simply said that he was away on business. We had a huge home, a housekeeper and a couple of maids, plus live-in bodyguards who watched over us. Once Finn and I got through the initial grief of losing our mother, we had a very happy adolescence. Cat would come and go, and his arrival home was always cause for celebration. Then he'd tell us where he'd been and what he'd done."

Jared dropped his foot to the floor and leaned forward, resting his elbows on his knees. "Are you telling me that Cat told two kids about . . ." He shook his head.

"About top-secret missions for the government? Yes. I'm sure he left out some of the more unpleasant details, but he did tell us. We knew it went no further than the three of us, but Cat said we were O'Caseys and we stuck together. He taught us how to use various weapons, how to scale walls, bypass intricate security systems, open combination safes, and on and on."

"Unbelievable."

She shrugged. "It seemed perfectly normal to us. It was what our father did when he wasn't home. As you probably know, he was independently wealthy, and Finn and I simply told our friends that Cat was away on business whenever he left. Cat told us he'd quit working for the government before he'd keep any secrets from us. He also said that what he was teaching us could be forgotten, or used for this country's good, whichever felt right to us."

"And?" Jared asked. "What did you and your brother decide when you became adults?"

"We chose not to become government agents."

"Thank God," Jared said under his breath. The knot that had tightened in his gut when he'd asked that question dissolved in a rush of relief. "Go on."

"Finn and I still live in the house in Beverly Hills in California. It's so big we have separate wings, like our own apartments. Both Finn and I inherited our mother's artistic talents. Finn is making a name for himself as a painter, and I have my own interior decorating firm. We had a good life, the three of us. Cat would come home and tell us what he'd done, then we'd get on with our lives. Your name became a household word. I felt as though I knew you, had known you for a long time. Cat said you were one of the best, and that you'd saved his life more than once. About five years ago he told us that you'd decided you'd had enough, and you were settling in here at Miracles. But he emphasized many times after that that you were the one Finn and I should come to if we were ever in trouble."

Jared laughed and leaned back in the chair. "Cat wrote his own rules, that's for sure. There'd be cardiac arrests in high places if it were known he was telling all to a couple of kids. Then he divulges the name and location of another agent? Holy hell. I've never told anyone outside of the agency or my street contacts about— But Cat was good. Damn, he was good. And he loved it, Tabor, every minute of it."

"I know," she said softly. "That's why he didn't quit when his health started to fail. Finn and I talked to him about it once . . . just once. He said he would die as he'd lived. He said that Finn and I had made our choices for our lives, and so had he. He said we had to love and respect each other enough to leave him alone, not nag and fuss at him about his health."

"So you kept quiet."

"Yes. It was so difficult, Jared, because we loved Cat so much. Then—"

There was a knock at the door.

"Dinner," Jared said, getting to his feet. He went to the door, pressed a button on the wall, and looked up at a small screen set above the door. The image of a white-coated waiter in his forties standing by a cart came into view. The waiter waggled his fingers and grinned. Jared opened the door.

"Come in, Trig," he said with a sigh. "You know, my highfalutin' security really loses something when you ham it up for the camera."

"Can't resist, boss," Trig said, pushing the cart

into the room. "I always wanted to be in show biz." He looked at Tabor. "Evening, ma'am. Enjoy your dinner. I have just delivered to you the finest meal—"

"Good-bye, Trig," Jared said.

"Oh, you bet. I'm gone. How do I look on camera, boss? Classy?"

"Uptown."

Trig grinned and left the room whistling. Chuckling, Jared began lifting the covers off the dishes of food.

"Trig," Tabor said thoughtfully. "Trigger Benson. He can shoot the wings off a fly."

Jared's head snapped up. Tabor smiled as she stood and walked over to him.

"You," he said, "are a bit disconcerting, Miss O'Casey. I don't think I want to know how much you know, or whom you know it about."

"No, I doubt that you do want to know. Mmm, that food looks delicious. Steak, lobster, baby carrots, rolls. Maybe I'm hungry after all."

Jared brought two straight-back chairs to the table, assisted Tabor with hers, then turned on softly glowing lights in the darkening room. He sat opposite Tabor, opened a bottle of wine, and filled her glass.

"Thank you," she said.

"Tabor, didn't Cat ever consider that he might be putting you and Finn in danger by telling you as much as he did?"

She swallowed a bite of steak. "This really is delicious, Jared. Thank you for going to all this trouble. To answer your question, no. No one would ever believe that two teenagers knew what we did. Then when Finn and I pursued our own careers . . . well, it simply wouldn't occur to anyone that we knew. You are now the only other person who knows."

"Only Cat would pull something like this. I wanted to go to his funeral, but it's not something we're supposed to do."

"I know. Cat had left specific instructions that it was to be a private service. It's still hard for me to realize that he's gone. I miss him so much."

"I'm sure you do," Jared said, covering her hand with his on the top of the table. "He was a hell of a man, Tabor. You can be very proud to be his daughter."

"He thought highly of you too, Jared," she said softly, looking directly into his eyes. "As I said, I feel as though I've known you for a long time." She wondered if that was why she'd responded to his kiss the way she had. Was it because she'd been waiting for so long to meet the great Jared Loring she'd heard about for years? Was that why being held and kissed by Jared had felt so right?

"I feel as though I've known you for a long time too, Tabor," he said. "That doesn't make sense in my case. Cat told me once that he had a couple of kids but never said more than that about you. I suppose it's our mutual link with Cat that makes me feel . . . well, it's not important." Or was it, he asked himself. Why did he feel so drawn to Tabor, so protective, so connected? He didn't know. "Go on with your story," he said, removing his hand from hers. "What brought you here? What's wrong?"

"Cat came home last month," Tabor said, pushing the food around her plate with her fork, "and he was very ill. He wouldn't let us call a doctor, just told Finn and me to listen carefully to what he said. He gave Finn a zippered black bag, one of those small ones like businesses use for making deposits. He also gave Finn a name and number of someone to call to say that Finn had what Cat had been sent for."

"Were you there? Did you see and hear all this?"

"Yes. Cat wanted Finn to do it, not me. Finn said he would, then I begged Cat to let us call a doctor. He refused. He smiled at us, told us we were the sunshine in his darkness, and—and he died."

"God. I'm sorry, Tabor."

"So am I," she said, managing a small smile.

"Did you understand what he meant when he said you were the sunshine in his darkness?"

"Yes." She blinked back her tears. "You're men of the night, of darkness, all of you who do that work. Cat told us that years ago, said that all of you referred to yourselves as men of the night. For him to call Finn and me his sunshine in that darkness was a precious gift to us."

"As it should be. It wasn't something that Cat would have said lightly."

"And you, Jared? Have you found your sunshine?"

"I have this casino. Tucker Boone and I own it."

"Is it enough? Is this enough sunshine?"

"We're getting off the subject," he said, dipping a bit of lobster into the dish of melted butter. Yes, he thought, Miracles was all the sunshine he needed. So why hadn't he said so? Hell, what difference did it make? "I assume Finn called the person Cat told him to."

"Yes. Finn was told on the phone to put the bag in a safe place and wait to be contacted. Weeks went by. Finn called the number again, but it had been disconnected. Three days ago he finally got a call and was told to meet a man named Mr. Blythe in warehouse four at the north shore docks at midnight, and to bring the bag."

"Back up here. What was the name of the man Finn first called?"

"Mr. Smith."

"Figures," Jared said gruffly. "Eat your dinner before it gets cold."

Tabor forced herself to take several more bites of the succulent lobster, then sipped her wine. "I wanted to go with Finn, but he said no."

"Good for him."

"I paced the floor after he left. Finn is big and in excellent condition, but he's an artist, for heaven's sake. It's one thing to be told how all this works while sitting in your own living room, and quite another to go out and do it."

"*You* did when you managed to get into this suite."

"I was desperate, Jared. I've been sick with worry. Finn called me that night about two A.M. He said he'd waited for Mr. Blythe but he never showed up. Finn decided to look around the other warehouses in case there'd been a mixup. He saw two men in the shadows in warehouse three. And he saw . . . a body on the floor. Finn told me that he thought it was a trap, that Blythe was probably the dead man, and a mixup of warehouse numbers had saved his own life. He said he'd come home and we'd figure out what to do next. Jared, he—"

"He what? Tabor?"

"He never came home." Her voice was thin and trembling. "Finn never came. I haven't heard a word from him, nothing. I didn't know what to do, and I couldn't sit there another minute. I came to you like Cat had always said I should. Oh, Jared, if they were watching me, if I've put you in danger by coming here, I—"

"Hey, hey, calm down. I've never made any secret of where I am. You didn't put me in any more danger than I've been in for the past five years since I became very visible here. Does Finn know I'm at Miracles?"

"Yes."

"Good. Do you know what was in the bag?"

"No, it had a small lock on it. It was soft, like papers, money—I don't know. We didn't care, we just wanted to keep our promise to our father. Oh, God, Jared, what has happened to Finn?"

"Tabor, listen to me and—"

"He didn't come home," she said, tears spilling onto her cheeks. "I waited . . . so many hours . . . and . . ."

"Tabor." He stood and walked around the table, then pulled her into his arms. She trembled against him as she cried. "Go ahead and cry," he said, stroking her hair. "You've earned a good cry. You've been through hell, but everything is going to be fine now, you'll see."

"I don't cry like this," she sobbed against his chest.

He smiled. "Of course, you don't. I know that, but until the rest of you remembers, I'll just hold you right here in my arms."

"I'm not crying. I'm not," she said as the tears continued to fall.

Jared tightened his hold on her slender body, gritting his teeth as she nestled against him, seeking solace. He fought the desire churning within him and concentrated on what Tabor had told him.

Everything was going to be fine? he asked himself dryly. Oh, yeah, sure. Piece of cake. Ha! Finn O'Casey had walked into a show starring the big-time boys, who had no second thoughts about blowing someone away. Damn that Cat O'Casey. No, that wasn't fair. Cat had included his children in all aspects of his life out of love. Not bright, but understandable. The delivery that Cat had sent Finn on should have gone without a hitch, and Cat's final job would have been completed as he'd wished. But there must have been a leak, some screwup, and now innocent people were in danger.

But, by damn, Jared vowed, nothing was going to happen to Tabor!

As for Finn, it didn't sound good. The more time that passed with no word from him, the greater the chance he was dead. Jared had to get some wheels in motion, start checking around to see what he could find out. He also had to ease Tabor away from his aching body before he passed out cold on the floor. How long did a woman at the end of her rope cry? He couldn't take much more of her pressed against him like this. He was about to explode.

"That's all, this is it," Tabor said, wiggling out of his arms. "I can't stand weeping women."

Thank the Lord, Jared thought.

"I apologize again for my tears," she said.

"No need." He handed her his handkerchief.

"Thank you." She dabbed at her nose, then lifted her chin. "There. Now. What do we do first to find my brother?"

"We?"

"You will help me, won't you?" she asked anxiously.

"Tabor, I'm not the half of the 'we' in question. Of course I'm going to find your . . . find out what happened to your brother. *You* aren't going to do a thing except be guarded twenty-four hours a day until I get a handle on what's going down."

"Jared, Finn is *my* brother."

"And you are *my* lady!"

Tabor frowned. "What?"

What? Jared asked himself. Where in hell had *that* come from? His body. Yes, it was because Tabor had been plastered against his aroused body while she cried. His mind had simply put into words the needs of his body. Oh, hell, he sounded like a shrink.

He raised his hands in a gesture of peace. "Let's cool down . . . I mean, calm down here, okay? Tabor, I know you want to do whatever you can to find Finn. You've done your part by coming to me. Now let me get started on this, all right?"

"Yes. Yes, of course. Thank you so much, Jared. You will let me help if I can, won't you? Cat trained me, remember?" She paused. "Jared, please answer me honestly. Do you think Finn is alive?"

"Hey, why would you think he—"

"Honestly, Jared. Please."

"I don't know, Tabor," he said quietly. "The more time that passes, the less I like it."

"One promise?"

"What is it?"

"Don't keep anything from me. Don't treat me like a child. I know I sobbed all over your shirtfront, but it won't happen again. Promise me, Jared, that I'll know exactly what is happening in regard to Finn. I can handle it. I'm an O'Casey."

More than an O'Casey, she was a woman, Jared thought. She was, in fact, like no woman he'd ever met before. She was soft and delicate, smelled like flowers, kissed like heaven, and was sending him over the edge with his desire for her. She had that special womanly wisdom that understood the cleansing and strengthening value of a good cry, an attribute a man could only envy. And in the next breath she had pulled herself together and demanded not to be protected from what could be a painful truth.

Oh, yes, Tabor O'Casey was all woman. He thought of how vehemently he had declared her to be his, and of how right those words had sounded as they hung heavily in the air. Something strange and foreign was happening to him in regard to Tabor.

"Jared?"

"I promise, Tabor," he said. "I won't keep anything from you. In exchange, you'll follow my orders just like everyone else I'm bringing in on this. Understood?"

She extended her hand. "You have a deal."

"Ma'am, I have no intention of shaking your hand to seal this deal. I'm going to kiss you to do that. I'm going to kiss you for a very long time."

"Oh," she said, dropping her hand to her side.

"But not now, because I have things to do. Hold the thought, though, and file it under unfinished deal sealing, or whatever."

"Oh," she said again.

He picked up the phone and pressed two buttons. "Mrs. Tuttle."

"Jared. We're going into Code Light Blue, Turtle."

"Hot damn!" she yelled. "We're all coming out of retirement."

"Turtle, I said Code *Light* Blue."

"Well, damn it all, I don't get a gun until Code Dark Blue. You're no fun, General Custer."

"Custer?"

"He wasn't the swiftest kid on the block either. Oh, well, we'll settle for Code Light Blue for now. Some of us have been waiting years for this, ever since we came to Miracles. Has to be a biggie to put you back into action, Jared. I know, I know, you'll tell me when you're ready to."

"Right. Issue guns to only the designated people on the Code Light Blue list. Get Nick, Trig, and Spider up here first though."

"Gotcha."

Jared replaced the receiver and crossed the room to the table he'd set his gun on. He clipped the holster back onto his belt, then shrugged into his jacket, leaving it unbuttoned. He opened the door, pushed the dinner cart into the hall, then stood in the doorway where he could see the full length of the corridor.

Incredible, Tabor thought, sinking into a chair. Jared had activated some kind of prearranged plan called Code Light Blue. He was surrounded by people ready to follow his orders without question. People of the night whom he shared the sunshine of Miracles with. People who were willing to step back into the night if he asked them to. And what of Jared himself? What was it costing him to do this for her five years after turning his back on it all? Was she taking too much from him? Would the price he'd pay be too high?

"Jared?"

"Yes?" he said, glancing over at her.

"Why are you doing this?"

"Because you asked me to."

"Is it because I'm Cat's daughter and Finn is his son?"

He looked down the corridor again. "That's half of it, I suppose."

"And the other half?"

"You. I'm doing it for you, but I don't have time right now to figure out why."

"I see," she said softly. "Am I asking too much of you? You left that dark world far behind you."

He sighed. "No one completely leaves it, not really. The memories are there, and the enemies. You're aware, I'm sure, that I had a very precise plan on hold in case something like this ever came up. This is the first time since I arrived at Miracles that I've put that plan into motion."

"You made a place here for a lot of people from your past, didn't you?"

"Carefully chosen ones. They weren't all agents. Some walked in places I'd never want you to see. But I know them, I trust them, and they trust me."

"But would you buy a used car from them?" she asked, smiling.

He looked at her again, matching her smile. "Not on your life."

"Trigger Benson wasn't an agent."

"No."

"He was a hit man for hire."

"I hauled his butt out of a tight spot once."

"So he owes you."

"No, Tabor, he trusts me. Big difference there."

"Spider," she said thoughtfully. "Spiderman Manchester, known for his daring leaps from building to building after robbing the rich of their fancy jewels. Copped a plea, did an assignment for the agency, then stayed on until he retired."

"Cat really gave you an education, didn't he?"

"To him, it was the same as any father telling his children about the people he knew and worked with. We didn't pass any judgment, we simply accepted what Cat told us as the way it was."

"Cat O'Casey was an unusual man."

"He was a loving father."

Jared nodded. "I realize that. I just hope . . . well, I hope Finn doesn't pay a heavy price for that love." He paused. "Come on, Turtle, get the message to those people."

"Turtle. Meredith Turtle Tuttle, master of disguises. Agent. Now you see her, now you don't."

"That's enough out of you, Miss Encyclopedia of the Grim and Grime. You're making me nervous with how much you know. I suppose Finn has all this great info in his brain too?"

"Yes."

"Dandy," Jared said, shaking his head. "Here they come off the elevator. Slow. That went much too slow."

"Don't say it, boss," Trig said as the men entered the room. "It was slow as molasses. I was serving a table in the restaurant and Spider and Nick waited for me. Are we really on Light Blue?"

"Yes."

"Never thought I'd see you put it into action," a tall, skinny man said. "I'm ready to fly."

"You're too old for that stuff, Spider," Trig said.

"Keep him on the ground, boss, or he'll break every bone in his bony body."

"Oh, ye of little faith," Spider said, clicking his tongue in disgust.

"Can it, gents," Jared said. "Nick, I called you up here to let you know we're in Code Light Blue. You're aware of who will now be legally carrying guns, and who might have to be replaced in the casino. If we go to Dark Blue, I'll let you know pronto. Beyond that, you're out of it, except for covering for me on the floor when I need you to. I'll try to get downstairs later tonight so you can get some sleep. I have no idea how long this will last. Okay?"

"No," Nick said.

"Did he say no to the boss?" Trig whispered to Spider.

"Shut up," Spider said. "I don't want to miss any of this."

"Do we have a problem here?" Jared asked Nick.

"Not really," Nick said. "When I came to work here a year ago you explained enough to me to give me a general picture of the setup. I knew I was to make adjustments as necessary should you ever pull employees out for the Code Blues. There wasn't any point in arguing about it at the time, as you made it clear that it might never happen. Well, it *has* happened. Jared, I realize I don't have the background your people do, or the training. But, dammit, you're all like family to me, and if something is going on, I have a right to do what I can to help that family."

"I'll be damned," Trig said. "That is really nice. Don't you think that's nice, Spider?"

"Yep. You're okay, Capoletti," Spider said. "Big too. Lots of muscle. Those types come in handy."

Jared ran his hand over the back of his neck. "I don't know, Nick. You can't even handle a gun."

"Wrong," Nick said. "You asked me if I wanted to wear a gun on the floor like you do, and I said no. Believe me, I can handle a gun. Jared, I want in."

"Mr. Capoletti," Tabor said, "maybe you should know that the situation being faced is because of me. I came here asking for Jared's help. So, you see, your family, as you call them, are once removed from the actual problem, unless they knew my father. You don't know me at all, nor are you accustomed to this sort of thing. I can't ask you to help me."

"I knew when I walked in here and saw that you were still with Jared that this all had to do with you. Jared has called a Code Light Blue alert. That's good enough for me."

"Well, okay," Jared said. "You win, Nick, but your primary responsibility is still going to be making sure the casino is covered as I assign employees to other tasks."

"That's fine," Nick said. "Just don't forget me when you're assigning."

"Let's sit down," Jared said. Everyone settled into chairs and onto the sofa. "Gentleman, this is Tabor O'Casey, daughter of the late and very great Cat O'Casey."

"Who?" Nick muttered.

"No joke? No joke?" Spider said. "The Cat's kid? No joke? Oh, that Cat was poetry in motion, something to behold in action. I remember the time—"

"Not now, Spider," Jared said. "Okay, listen up. Cat O'Casey felt his children had the right to know who he really was and what he did for the government. So . . ."

Tabor watched as Jared explained what had taken place and where things now stood with Finn. The other men were listening intently, she saw, missing no detail. They would do whatever Jared asked of them, she knew, out of respect and trust. And, as Nick had said, because they were family. Jared was their leader. A stranger would know that the instant he walked into the room. His aura of authority and power made it perfectly clear who was in charge.

And if a woman entered the room? Despite Nick's exceptional good looks, Tabor knew she would be drawn immediately to Jared, to his raw sensuality and masculinity. More than dangerous, Jared Loring was exciting and magnificent.

"Don't sound good for Finn O'Casey, boss," Trig said. He glanced at Tabor. "Oh, hey, I'm sorry. I shouldn't have said that. You'd be surprised at the tight spots people can wiggle out of."

"Tabor realizes that her brother is in danger," Jared said. "That's why she's here. She could be in jeopardy too. I don't know yet. Fact is, I don't know anything yet. Nick, I want Pico and Joe outside my door on rotating shifts. Tabor, you don't leave this suite until I give the word."

"I can't stay here," she said. "What I mean is, don't you have another room I can use?"

"You're safer in this one," Nick said.

Oh, really? Tabor thought. Safe from outside danger, perhaps. But who was going to protect her from the desire that flared instantly when Jared touched her? Who was going to protect her from him, and, even more, from herself?

"Trig," Jared said, "get on the streets, see what the word is. Maybe the guys who took out the fed on the coast were hired in for the job. You know what to do, cover all the angles."

"I'm gone," Trig said, and a moment later he was.

"Spider," Jared said, "talk to your old buddies. Whenever Cat O'Casey did a job, everyone sat around talking about what a class act it was."

"Yep," Spider said as he headed for the door. "We'll find your brother, Miss O'Casey. Don't fret about it none."

"Thank you, Spider," Tabor said.

"I'm going to make some calls, see what I can dig up," Jared said after Spider left. "There are a few people who owe me favors. Nick, take care of covering Trig's and Spider's spots, get Pico and Joe set up, then get yourself a gun from Turtle. I'll be down to take the floor as soon as I get off the phone."

Nick nodded and left.

"And me?" Tabor asked.

"Do you have a picture of Finn?"

"Yes, in my wallet."

"Keep it for now. I'll know you have it if we need it."

"What else can I do?" she asked.

"Nothing, until we start piecing this thing together." He paused and looked directly at her. "Are you all right?"

"Yes, and very grateful to you, Jared. Your people are wonderful too."

"There are a lot of others in this world who wouldn't find anything wonderful about Trig or Spider, or me, for that matter. I've killed men when I had no other choice, Tabor."

"So did my father. He killed when it meant he would stay alive and come home to us. He killed only those trying to kill him, and he said that was how you operated too. Jared, if you're trying to shock me by referring to what you did while you were an agent, it's impossible. I grew up knowing of these things, remember? Even more, I learned to understand why it was all so important, why it had to be done. I also know that my brother is in a great deal of danger. I'm doing the best I can with that."

Jared slowly stood up. "You're a remarkable woman."

"No, I'm a desperately frightened woman, and I'm hanging on by a thread because I'm so worried about Finn."

"We'll do everything we can, I promise you that."

"I know you will, Jared," she said softly. "I'm just like the others, you see. I trust you."

"I haven't earned your trust, Tabor."

She stood as well and crossed the room to him. She framed his face with her hands, then reached up and brushed her lips over his.

"Yes, you have," she said. "You've earned my trust. And, Jared? I am truly grateful to you for all you're doing about Finn." She stepped back. "I know you have calls to make."

"Yes, I do," he said, resisting the urge to pull her into his arms. "I'll make them in the bedroom, then let you know what I find out. That will give you a chance to relax out here. You've had a rough day. If anyone knocks at the door, come get me. Don't open it yourself."

"All right."

He drew his thumb across her lips, then turned and walked into the bedroom, a frown knitting his brow. Truly grateful, he repeated in his mind. It made sense that she was relieved she was no longer alone to face the problem of Finn's disappearance. But she kept saying thank you, kept expressing her gratitude.

He closed the door and sat down on the edge of his king-size bed. He ran his hands over his face, but his frown remained.

What was the problem, he asked himself. Tabor's gratitude was totally understandable. But, dammit, he didn't want her gratitude! That wasn't at all what he wanted from her. That last sensuous touch of her lips on his had made his blood run hot in his veins. Had that been nothing more than her way of saying thank you?

And what about the earlier kiss? No, he thought, that had been real and unexpected passion exploding in him, and in her. But now he felt something had shifted off-center. Tabor seemed to be more grateful to him than anything else, and for reasons he couldn't begin to explain, that made him feel cheated, angry, frustrated, and . . . lonely.

"Ah, hell, forget it," he said, lunging to his feet.

He lifted a painting down from one wall and opened the safe hidden behind it. From inside he took a small black book, then returned to the bed. He set the book on the pillow and placed his hand on the phone. In the next instant he was on his feet again, walking to the door and yanking it open.

Tabor was standing by the window staring out at the bright lights of Las Vegas that beckoned to all to enter this world of fantasy. She looked up quickly at the sound of the door opening, a questioning expression on her face as she watched Jared stride toward her.

"Jared, what is—"

"Unfinished business," he said gruffly.

"Pardon me?"

"I said I wouldn't shake your hand to seal our deal, remember?"

"Yes, but . . ."

He wove his fingers through her hair to hold her head steady, then lowered his head to hers. "We'll do it my way."

It was all and more than the first kiss had been. The embers of desire that still glowed within them burst into a raging fire. Their tongues met as their bodies pressed close, seeking, aching. The kiss was urgent, frenzied, equally shared. Their hearts pounded, their breathing became labored as currents of heat wove back and forth between them, igniting their passions further.

Jared lifted his head. "That," he said hoarsely, "was you and me. Just you and me. It had nothing to do with your brother or your damn gratitude. Understand?"

"Why are you so angry?" she whispered.

"Answer me. That kiss was us. Do you understand that, Tabor?"

"Yes, but . . ."

"Good." He stepped away and started back toward the bedroom. "Don't forget it." He closed the door behind him with a thud.

Tabor sank into a chair and stared at the closed door. She pressed her fingertips to her throbbing lips and willed her heart to return to a normal cadence.

What on earth was *that* all about, she wondered. Jared shifted moods so quickly she couldn't keep up. His anger, his words, didn't make sense. As for the kiss . . . She'd dissolved in his arms, answered every demand of his mouth, and had wanted more.

Of course she was grateful to Jared for what he was doing to help her, she reasoned, but that had nothing to do with her attraction to him, her response to his kisses. *Your damn gratitude,* Jared had said. Her being grateful made him angry? This was terribly confusing. Her mind was becoming a jumbled maze of thoughts about Finn, and Jared, and . . .

But one thing was becoming clear, she decided, still staring at the closed door. Jared Loring was a very, very complicated man.

Three

An hour later Jared emerged from the bedroom, and Tabor was instantly on her feet.

"Nothing yet," he said. "I'm trying to get in touch with people I haven't seen or spoken to in five years. It's not that easy to do. I have to relieve Nick on the floor, but I'll be up later to check on you. Pico or Joe will be right outside. I saw your suitcase in the bedroom. If you get tired, go to bed in there. I'll sleep out here on the sofa."

"No, I'll take the sofa."

"You're safer in there, Tabor. There's no way to get into the bedroom except through here."

"Do you really think I'm in danger?"

He frowned. "I don't know. Hell, I don't know anything at this point. Turtle will page me on the floor if any of my calls are returned. Trig and Spider will check in later, and we'll see what we have. This is not the way I like to operate, but . . . we wait."

"You'd rather be doing instead of waiting, wouldn't you?"

"Yes, I certainly would. I've got to go. You're safe here, Tabor."

"I know," she said softly, "and I'm very . . ."

Their gazes collided and Tabor saw the flash of anger in Jared's eyes, then something else she couldn't decipher. She'd been about to say *grateful*, but had caught herself at the last second. She knew Jared had realized what she was going to say, and his anger had flared once again. Why? Why couldn't she express her thanks for all he was doing for her?

"Make yourself at home," he said, starting toward the door.

"Jared?"

"Yes?" He turned slightly to look at her.

"Nothing. I'll be fine," she said, forcing a smile. "You have an entire wall of books over there. I'll find something to read."

"There's a panel of buttons by that closed door in the middle of the bookshelves. There's a wide-screen television behind it, a VCR, a stereo."

"Goodness, so much to pick from. Don't give me another thought."

He studied her for a long moment. "Right," he said dryly, then continued on to the door and opened it.

"Mr. Loring," a deep voice said.

"Hello, Pico. No one goes in this room except me or Nick. And no one comes out."

"Yes, sir."

Jared closed the door with a decisive click that seemed to echo loudly in the silent room. Tabor shivered despite the perfectly controlled temperature, and wandered over to the bookshelves. Jared's taste in reading varied greatly, she soon realized. He had many leather-bound editions of the classics, several shelves of science fiction and mysteries, non-fiction books about history and psychology, and rows and rows of novels of all kinds that had been on the best-seller list. An illustrated book about old castles around the world intrigued her, and she slipped out of her shoes and curled up in the corner of the sofa with the book on her lap.

Before she opened it, though, she looked around the room. Jared's suite, she decided, had none of the sterile sameness she always associated with hotels. It was an apartment, a home, expensively furnished, and with original paintings on the walls. The rich hues of burgundy and blue were masculine, as was the large furniture. Yet the room was also inviting, warm, offering comfort to those who entered.

Her gaze was drawn to the open doorway leading to Jared's bedroom. She was to sleep in his huge bed, she mused, while he stretched out on the sofa she was now sitting on. Jared Loring, she was very sure, was not accustomed to sleeping on the sofa when a woman was spending the night in his suite.

What kind of lover was he, she wondered. Demanding? Yes. Would the strength evident in his powerful body be tempered with gentleness? Oh, yes. He would give as much as he took, sharing the pleasure of that most intimate act. To become one with Jared, she somehow knew, would be glorious, like nothing she'd experienced before. It would be special and—

Stop it, Tabor, she told herself firmly. She couldn't believe she was sitting there fantasizing about sharing a bed with a man she'd known only for a handful of hours. Yet, when he'd kissed her she'd wanted him with a driving force. It hadn't been a helpless surrendering to expert seduction, but a feeling of rightness, of having waited a long time to find and become one with this incredible man.

She knew none of this was like herself, how she usually behaved or thought. But she had never before met a man like Jared Loring. She'd had an image in her mind of Jared for years, but could no longer remember how she'd pictured him in her imagination. The real Jared was larger than life, and had superimposed himself over quickly fading mental shadows. Jared was Jared, and she had been changed from the moment she saw him.

Tabor pressed her fingertips to her now throbbing temples and closed her eyes. So much had happened, she thought, and all so quickly. She felt fragmented, pulled between her heartrending worry for Finn and the heightened awareness of herself in regard to Jared. She had to settle down, get a grip on herself, concentrate on the mission of finding her brother.

She needed a bath, she decided, setting the book aside. She'd take a long, leisurely bath and relax, just blank her mind and let the tension ebb from her body.

She stood up and walked into the bedroom. She glanced at the bed, refused to think, and hurried on to the large bathroom.

On the bustling floor of the casino Jared found Nick talking to a tall, attractive brunette in a gold lamé dress. The woman looked at Jared, did a double take at his stern expression, then left hurriedly, mumbling good-bye to Nick.

"Sorry about that," Jared said to Nick.

"You scared her to death," Nick said, chuckling. "That's okay. She was only after my body. I want to be respected for my brilliant mind."

"Bull."

Nick laughed, but when Jared's expression remained stony, he quickly sobered.

"Bad news?" he asked.

"No news," Jared said. "Everything is in motion, but there's no feedback yet. I'm not high on standing around and waiting. Did Turtle take care of issuing guns to those who are supposed to have them?"

"Yes. Everything is under control." Nick paused. "This is an incredible situation, like something out of a movie. I realize it's old hat to you, but this gun I'm wearing feels like a bowling ball. There's a woman in your suite who might be in danger, a man has been kidnapped or worse, a secret plan of yours has been activated. . . . This is heavy stuff. What do you think the chances are that Finn O'Casey is alive?"

"Not good. It would be different if they'd gotten their hands on Cat, but Finn was just a messenger. I doubt it would ever occur to them that he knows as much as he does. Of course, there's always the possibility that . . ." Jared's voice trailed off.

"That what?" Nick asked, leaning toward him.

"Finn O'Casey is, in essence, an innocent citizen. The agency is big on keeping those types safe and alive, and everyone knows that. He could be a pawn, being held with the idea of trading him for something, or someone. They already have, I assume, whatever Finn was delivering. If he's still alive, there's a definite reason why."

Nick shook his head. "I'm having a hard time believing all of this. Lord, Jared, it's going to be rough on Tabor if her brother has been killed carrying out their dead father's final wishes."

"I know," Jared said quietly.

"How is she holding up?"

A small smile touched Jared's lips. "She's something. She's tough as nails one minute, then crying all over my shirt the next, even while she's telling me she can't tolerate weeping women. She's strong yet vulnerable, and she's being brave even though she's badly frightened. As beautiful as she is, she could pull a helpless routine and everyone would fall over their feet to comfort and protect her, but she isn't doing that. Tabor is in there pitching, wants to do her part to get her brother. . . ." Jared glanced at Nick. "What are you grinning about?"

"Grinning? Me?" Nick asked, all innocence. His smile grew even bigger. "I'm listening to every word you're saying, Jared. Why would I be grinning?"

"I sure as hell don't know," Jared said with disgust. "All I was doing was answering your question about how Tabor was doing."

"Beautiful Tabor," Nick said. "You did say she was beautiful."

"So? I'm sure you figured that out the minute you saw her."

Nick shrugged. "She's okay, I guess."

"Are you nuts?" Jared quickly looked around, then lowered his voice. "Or blind? She's sensational, Capoletti. I have never in my life seen such gorgeous hair. And her face, her figure. She's . . . why am I having this conversation with you?"

"We're chatting," Nick said pleasantly. "People do that, you know. They chat. We're standing here chatting about the fact that Tabor O'Casey is turning you inside out."

"She is not!"

At least a dozen people stopped what they were doing and stared at Jared.

"You were saying?" Nick asked, raising his eyebrows.

"Nothing," Jared muttered. "I wasn't saying a damn word to you, Capoletti. You're so insane, it's pathetic. Go away. I'm on floor duty now."

"I think I'll hang around awhile, see if anything develops about Finn O'Casey."

"Fine. Do whatever you want. Just don't talk to me."

"Yes, sir," Nick said as Jared strode away. "I read you loud and clear, sir."

Jared smiled and nodded at a group of people he passed, and hoped his forced, friendly expression appeared sincere.

Nick was crazy, he thought. Tabor O'Casey was turning him, Jared Loring, inside out? Not a chance. There wasn't a woman born who could get to him the way Nick was insinuating. Not even a woman as beautiful as Tabor, with hair like Tabor's, a face and body like Tabor's. Not even though she kissed like a dream, felt like heaven when he held her in his arms, and the mere thought of her caused him to ache with the want of her.

"Damn," he mumbled, "she *is* turning me inside out."

"Were you speaking to me, Mr. Loring?" a cocktail waitress asked.

"What? Oh, no, Donna, I wasn't."

"Darn," the woman said, and continued on her way.

Jared strolled through the casino, not really seeing what he was looking at. His mind was centered on Tabor. Had she gone to bed? It was after midnight, and she'd had a grueling day. Was she at that very moment curled up asleep in his bed, her hair spread out like a golden halo over the pillow? If he kissed her awake would she lift her arms in welcome, or launch into another spiel about how grateful she was for his help?

And that was another thing, Jared mentally fumed on. Why had it bothered him that Tabor had apparently begun to regard him as only a means to an end, a hero who was going to rescue her brother? Why did it matter so much that in her eyes he was a man, a man in relationship to her as a woman?

What was Tabor O'Casey doing to him?

That question taunted Jared as he checked in with the cashiers, watched the dealers change tables in their regular rotation procedure, saw a man lose five thousand dollars at the roulette wheel and a woman win ten thousand.

What was Tabor doing to him? He didn't know, but he didn't like it, and whatever it was, it was going to stop. Now. From that moment forward Tabor was part of an assignment he hadn't asked for but would carry through to its end. She was Cat O'Casey's daughter, and he was seeing to her welfare and, he hoped, the return of her brother as a final gift to a departed friend. Fine. Everything was once more under control. *His* control.

He was standing near the blackjack tables when Nick approached him.

"Heard anything?" Nick asked.

"No," Jared said. "Nothing."

"Well, it's after two. I guess I'll get some sleep. Wake me up if anything happens, or if you need me."

"Okay. These things take time, Nick. Trig and Spider have to find their sources on the street. The people I sent word to could be anywhere. The problem is, we don't know how much time Finn has . . . if any."

"Wait, Jared. Look. Spider just came in the front door."

"Good. Let's hope he found out something."

Spider gazed across the casino at Jared and Nick, and Jared nodded slightly to the right. Spider headed that way, and Jared and Nick followed at a leisurely pace.

Their destination was a small office off a corridor beyond the gaming floor. Jared unlocked the door, and the trio entered. He turned on the lamp on the desk, then leaned against the desk and looked at Spider.

"Any luck?" he asked.

"Of course," Spider said. "I always get the job done. Cat O'Casey pulled off the coup of the decade. He snatched a list of names of very wealthy, very important U.S. citizens who are involved in selling guns to little countries who shouldn't have that kind of toy. The list is complete; not just names, but dates, amounts of money, where the guns were bought, and where they were shipped to."

"Good Lord," Nick said.

"Cat was the best," Spider went on. "The safe he got the list out of was fifteen floors up in a swanky apartment in Los Angeles. Cat went right up the side of the building."

There was a soft knock at the door, and Nick answered it. Trig entered.

"It's big, boss," Trig said without a usual greeting.

"So I hear," Jared said. "Gun running."

"Yep. You find out about the list, Spider?"

Spider sniffed indignantly. "Of course."

"What I haven't heard," Jared said, "is who the list was stolen from."

"I don't know," Spider said. "My sources were all hyped up over the fact that Cat was able to scale that building and get it. I didn't hear any names."

"I did," Trig said. "The safe was in the apartment of a certain Mickey 'the Mouse' Mason."

Jared straightened from the desk and cut loose with a few earthy expletives.

"Mickey the Mouse?" Nick repeated. "Some guy is really called Mickey the Mouse? Do these people stay up at night thinking about what to name themselves?"

"No, no, Nick," Spider said. "That's what Mickey Mason is referred to on the streets. The last idiot who said it to his face ended up in the morgue. I mean, would you want to be called Mickey 'the Mouse' Mason?"

"Not particularly," Nick said. "He's a scum, huh?"

"A peach of a guy," Jared said. "He's into guns, drugs, prostitution, anything illegal and profitable. The feds have been after him for years but can't get a thing on him to use in court. Cat got the list that could have done it, but the Mouse obviously got it back."

"Wrong," Trig said.

"What?"

"I don't know details, boss, but the word is that the Mouse's muscle snuffed the fed who was to meet Cat O'Casey's kid. They snatched Finn O'Casey and the bag, but . . ." He shrugged.

"Spit it out, Trigger," Spider said. "You're being a showboat."

"You're a dud, Spider," Trig said.

"Trig," Jared said in an ominous voice, "I'm waiting."

"Oh, sure thing, boss," Trig said quickly. "Just feels so good to be back in action, you know what I mean?"

"Trigger, now."

"Oh. Well, like I said, I don't have all the scoop on how or what, but when Finn O'Casey was delivered to the Mouse with the bag, all that was in the pouch were pages from a telephone book. Mason didn't get his list back, boss, and there's no word out on what happened to Finn."

Jared's next string of expletives was even more fierce. He ran his hand over the back of his neck, narrowed his eyes, and stared at a spot on the far wall. No one spoke as they looked at him. Several minutes passed.

"Cat O'Casey," Jared finally said, directing his gaze to the three men, "would never have pulled a switch. He sent his son on what should have been a quick, easy drop. Finn played it cozy, saw that it was a setup, and called Tabor to fill her in. He said he was coming home, and they'd figure out what to do next. He never arrived. Between the time that Finn called Tabor and was starting home, things went bad."

"He smelled a rat," Spider said.

"A mouse," Nick said. "Sorry. I just can't believe that guy's moniker. Go ahead, Jared."

"The way I see it," Jared went on, "Finn realized they were on to him, but he had enough time to stash the list and make the switch before they got him. The question is, where did he put the list? And how long can he hold out against Mason's muscle before he tells them?"

"Then you figure that Finn is alive?" Nick asked.

"If he hasn't talked, he is. Nick, have Jerry cover the casino floor, then you three get some sleep. I'm going to see if Tabor can remember anything about that call from Finn to give us more clues. First, though, I'll press my contacts and find out if Mason is still sweating because he doesn't have the list. If he's happy as a clam, then . . . damn."

"Finn O'Casey is dead meat," Trig said. "We're racing against time, boss."

"That Finn O'Casey is something, isn't he?" Spider said. "What a gutsy move. His daddy would be proud of him. Yeah, he's something, that Finn."

"So is his sister," Jared said, starting toward the door.

Nick suppressed a smile by clearing his throat.

"Trig, Spider," Jared said, glancing back at them, "you did a nice job."

"Of course," Spider said, "but thank you."

"We're not done," Trig said. "We have to get Finn out of the Mouse's hands—fast."

"No joke," Jared said sarcastically. He gripped the

doorknob tighter than was necessary. "If Finn won't talk, Mason may try to get the leverage he needs to convince Finn to change his mind."

Nick's eyes widened. "Tabor," he whispered.

"Yeah," Jared said, a muscle jumping along his jaw. "Tabor."

The four men exchanged long looks, then Jared left the office. He swiftly crossed the casino, his mind echoing Tabor's name. If Finn wouldn't talk, Mason would come after Tabor.

Hot fury twisted within Jared as he stepped out of the elevator on the upper floor. No one, he vowed, was going to hurt Tabor O'Casey. He was going to protect her, keep her safe. To get to Tabor, Mickey Mason would have to go over, through, or around Jared Loring, and that wasn't going to happen.

Jared entered the large office that he shared with Nick, and sat down behind the desk. As he reached for the telephone, he was unaware that his blue eyes were as cold as chips of ice.

Forty-five minutes later Jared greeted Pico, standing guard at the suite. Once inside, Jared locked the door and shrugged out of his jacket.

He'd found out what he needed to know. Mickey Mason did not have the list.

They were always there, Jared mused as he walked to the bar. The voices in the night, the shadows in the darkness. People who were willing to speak, tell what they knew, for a price. Jared's reputation had held him in good stead. He'd been told what he needed, and his sources knew that the money he promised them would reach them before dawn's light, before the darkness faded and they scurried to take cover.

Jared splashed some Scotch into a glass and took a hefty swallow. The night was his world, he thought, the one he understood and accepted. Five years ago he'd tempered the harshness of the darkness with Miracles, his sunshine, his home. Yet when Tabor had asked him if Miracles provided enough sunshine, he hadn't answered her. He'd avoided answering her question because he'd been struck by an unexpected flicker of doubt. Damn her! It was as though she refused to leave any part of his life untouched by her disturbing presence.

He drained his glass and stared across the room at the half-closed door to the bedroom.

He was, he admitted, postponing going into that bedroom and seeing Tabor asleep in his bed. The mere image of her lying there was enough to cause a potent heat to pour through his body. There he stood, big, tough Jared Loring, scared to confront a woman, a woman who captivated him as no other, made him ache with a desire he'd never felt before, and caused him to lose his once unshakable control.

"Move, Loring," he muttered, and crossed the room to push the door open.

The soft light from the living room lamps cast a rosy glow over the bed. Jared walked slowly forward, the thudding of his heart actually painful in his chest. He stopped by the edge of the bed and shoved trembling hands into his pockets as he gazed down at the vision of loveliness before him.

Tabor.

She was lying on her back, her golden hair spread out over the pillow. One hand was curled next to her cheek while her other arm was flung out beside her, as though she'd been searching for something, or someone, on the opposite side of the big bed. The blankets were pulled only to her waist, revealing a thin-strapped pale pink satin nightgown with a scooped neck and a pink ribbon tied beneath her full breasts. She was exquisite.

Jared's hands curled into tight fists as he struggled against the urge to touch her, to draw her close to his aching body and cover her lips with his.

Dear Lord, how he wanted her.

He would skim the satin nightgown from her soft skin, shed his clothes, and love her until she was ready for him. Then he would drive his throbbing manhood deep within her welcoming warmth. He would be one with Tabor.

She had said, he remembered, that she felt as though she'd known him for a long time due to Cat's telling everything to his children. But why did he, Jared, feel the same strange sensation about Tabor, that he knew her with a depth that came from years spent together instead of from the few hours it had been? Why was there such a . . . a peacefulness within him, coexisting with his raging desire? A peacefulness that said that the time had come to make love with this woman in a joining that would be special, rare, beautiful.

Why was this little voice whispering that Tabor O'Casey was his sunshine?

Jared shook his head abruptly. What was wrong with him? He felt as if he were watching himself from afar, seeing himself split in two. Half of him was a man aching for this woman, the other a man filled with warmth and sunshine because she was there. He didn't understand what was happening, and that was unacceptable. He must regain control of himself.

Tabor stirred in her sleep, her outstretched hand moving restlessly over the empty expanse of bed next to her. She murmured one word in a sleep-husky voice. One word that caused Jared to stifle a moan as the blood pounded in his veins. One word. Jared.

He closed his eyes for a moment and drew in a deep breath before he looked at her again. His hands ached from the tight fists he'd curled them into, and he forced them to open, pulling them from his pockets.

He had to wake her, but standing as he was beside the bed, she'd have a clear view of his shameless arousal. She'd probably leap off the bed and deck him with the lamp on the nightstand.

But, oh, Lord, the way she'd said his name had turned his blood to liquid fire. Her arm lying across the bed made him yearn to stretch out next to her to be found by her searching fingers. Was she dreaming about him? Had a dream of their making love prompted that sensual whispering of his name?

Dammit, Jared thought, he was driving himself crazy with these fantasies. He had to wake Tabor and ask her about the telephone call she'd received from Finn. So he'd wake her. *After* he figured out how to hide the evidence of his body's reaction to her.

A straight-back chair stood against the wall, and he carried it to the bed. He sat down, leaned forward to rest his elbows on his knees, and laced his hands loosely together.

That, he decided dryly, was as good as it was going to get.

"Tabor," he said. "Tabor, wake up."

She moved her head on the pillow but didn't open her eyes.

"Tabor, it's Jared."

Tabor stood alone in the misty fog, frantically searching for Jared. She had to find him. Her father had walked past her, nodding in approval as she called Jared's name. Finn had been there, too, but he hadn't stayed. He'd hurried on as though he were eager to get someplace else. But she couldn't find Jared!

She'd been waiting a lifetime for him, and she knew that this night was theirs, the one when they would make love, beautiful love. But the fog had come instead of Jared, and their chance would be lost if this night passed without their becoming one. It was the law of the darkness. The arrival of the sunshine had to be timed perfectly. Oh, she had to find her Jared.

"Tabor."

His voice. She could hear the rich velvet timbre of his voice.

"Tabor, it's Jared."

She slowly opened her eyes, aware at once that the fog was gone in this new place she was searching. She didn't know where she was, but maybe Jared was there. Maybe he had called to her to come there because he was waiting for her, because he, too, knew this was their special night. She turned her head.

"Oh, Jared," she whispered as she saw him. Her hands floated up and toward him. "At last I've found you. Come to me. Don't leave me again. Please. Love me. This is our night."

A rushing noise filled Jared's ears, and his heart thundered. Rational thought fled. Before he knew it he was moving from the chair to the bed, his hands tangling in Tabor's hair as her arms circled his neck.

He lowered his head and kissed her.

His tongue delved into her mouth, and she met it with her own, eagerly, hungrily. They drank each other's sweetness like thirsty souls finding the nectar that would sustain them. Heat and desire consumed them, passion flaring into a roaring fire of want and need.

Jared trailed kisses across the silky skin of her shoulders, then down to the tops of her breasts, pushing above the satin nightgown. His hands slid the thin straps of the gown away, and she dropped her arms from his neck to allow him to lower the material down to her waist, baring her breasts to his smoldering gaze.

"Beautiful," he murmured, his Southern accent once again more pronounced than usual. "So beautiful . . . and mine."

He dipped his head to draw the sensitive bud of one breast into his mouth, his tongue stroking the nipple to a taut button. He sucked, he sipped. He savored and tasted as though sampling a secret wine that he alone would ever know of. He moved to her other breast to repeat the tantalizing foray, and a purr of pleasure escaped from Tabor's lips.

With obvious reluctance Jared left the lush bounty

of Tabor's breasts, then stood to remove her night-gown. She was naked before him, the soft light from the living room casting muted hues over her dewy skin. A tightness closed his throat, and he made no attempt to speak as he gazed raptly at every inch of her. Finally he met her eyes, and they were dark with desire, asking him to come to her.

He shed his clothes, his fingers fumbling, trembling, as he worked the gold studs free from his shirt. Then he stood by the bed naked, fully aroused, his muscles tensing as Tabor's gaze slowly traveled over him. He felt vulnerable, desperately needing the approval of this woman who would receive all that he was as a man into the warm, sweet haven of her body.

He was magnificent, Tabor thought dreamily. Jared was beautifully proportioned, with muscles taut beneath his tanned skin. The hair on his chest was a silvery glow of curls, his shoulders wide, his hips narrow. And he wanted her. His manhood was a bold announcement of that.

"Magnificent," she whispered. "You are the most beautiful man I've ever seen. Love me, Jared. Now. I want you so much."

The little voice in Jared's mind yelled at him that he was out of control, that his actions were dictated by emotions and needs he couldn't even name. He'd come to that room to . . . to talk to Tabor about the telephone call from Finn, to . . .

She lifted one hand to him. "Please, Jared."

He was lost. The groan that rumbled from his throat drowned out the voice in his mind. There was only Tabor and his burning desire for her.

He moved onto the bed, over her, then into her.

She arched her back to receive him, all of him, so deeply within her.

He captured her mouth in a hard kiss, then lifted his head to watch her face. She met his gaze, a soft smile touching her lips.

He began to move inside her, and she rose to meet him. The rhythm was wild, pounding. Tension built within their bodies, coiling, tightening, as they struggled to the summit of a climb of ecstasy.

"Jared!"

Spasms swept through her in waves, and a moment later he surged one last time within her, spilling his life force into her womanly darkness. He collapsed against her, his breathing rough. Their bodies were slick with perspiration, and minutes passed as their heartbeats quieted.

The little voice called to Jared, and he felt as though he were returning to his own body after being hurled to an unknown place. The voice hammered at him, demanded an explanation for his losing control, for not staying on a straight course to complete the mission of finding Finn O'Casey.

The voice asked, but Jared had no answers.

He lifted himself away from Tabor and rolled onto his back, flinging an arm across his eyes. His mind was a maze of confusion, and he felt drained, exhausted. The lovemaking he had just shared with Tabor had been as special, as beautiful as he'd known it would be. But before he could savor it, it was being pushed into the shadows, the warmth of its sunshine blocked by the darkness.

Tabor blinked and took a deep, steadying breath. A dream, she told herself. It had all been a dream. The fog . . . searching for Jared . . . then . . .

She turned her head to look at the man lying so still beside her. No, she thought, not a dream. It had been lovemaking so incredibly beautiful there would never be words rich enough to describe it. Her body still hummed with glorious sensations and a sweet aching in tender places. It had started as a dream, then had quickly become wondrous reality. She wasn't sorry; she would never regret sharing what she had with Jared Loring.

"I'm sorry," he said quietly, his arm still covering his eyes.

"What?" she asked, staring at him with wide eyes.

"That shouldn't have happened. You were half asleep . . . I should have called a halt before . . . Sorry doesn't cut it, but I don't know what else to say. I woke you to ask you about Finn, not to seduce you. Ah, dammit." He flung his arm out and his fist pounded the bed.

"I'm not sorry, Jared," she said softly. "It was beautiful between us, very special."

"Yes, it was, but you didn't know what you were doing until it was too late to stop. You were dreaming, weren't you? About me? You said my name. You thought you were still dreaming when you reached out to me, right? Right, Tabor?"

"Yes, but . . ."

He swung his feet to the floor and sat up, his back to her. He ran his hand down his face and shook his head.

"Lord, I can't believe I did this," he said, a rough edge to his voice. "I don't know what happened. I just . . ." He stood up. "I'm truly sorry, Tabor. I'll take a quick shower, then I've got to ask you some questions about Finn." He started across the room.

Tabor sat up. "I said I wasn't sorry. I have no regrets about what happened."

He stopped at the bathroom door and turned to look at her. "You will when you really think about *how* it happened, how I seduced you, how you didn't realize what you were doing." He laughed a sharp, bitter laugh. "Well, this ought to take care of that overabundance of gratitude you had. I solved that problem in spades." He went into the bathroom and slammed the door behind him.

"Oh, Jared," she whispered, unexpected tears misting her eyes. "You're wrong. I'll never regret this night. Never."

Four

When Jared came out of the bathroom with a towel tucked around his hips, Tabor wasn't in the bedroom. Panic flashed through him, then he realized she couldn't have left the suite. Pico or Joe were stationed outside the door.

Wonderful, he thought, reaching in the dresser drawer for clean clothes. Jared Loring had resorted to holding a woman in his room, possibly against her will. Jared Loring had also seduced a woman who was so groggy with sleep she hadn't known what she was doing. Despite what Tabor had said, she would come to despise him for what he'd done.

He pulled on jeans and a blue knit shirt, clipped his gun to the back of his belt, then stepped back into the bathroom to comb his hair. Forcing himself to meet his eyes in the mirror, he called himself a few less than flattering names.

He'd really blown it, he thought as he put on his shoes and socks. What had happened in that bed with Tabor seemed like a dream, something removed from reality. Their lovemaking had been precious, like none he'd experienced before. Tabor had been so passionate, so responsive to his every kiss and touch. She'd given as much as she'd received, holding nothing back, trusting him. She'd taken him to a height of ecstasy he hadn't known existed, soaring with him every inch of the way.

Lord, how he'd wanted her. And still wanted her. He'd never get enough of Tabor O'Casey.

Jared glanced at the bed. A dream? he mused. No, it had been real, wonderfully real, but his fear now was that his actions would haunt him like a nightmare. Tabor would feel used, seduced and used. She'd come to him for help because her brother was in trouble, then . . . damn.

Shaking his head in disgust, Jared walked into the living room. Tabor was sitting on the sofa, a matching satin robe covering her pink nightgown. She'd tied her hair at the nape of her neck with a pink ribbon. Her back was to him, her head slightly bent. She seemed small and vulnerable, and his heart wrenched painfully.

What was she thinking, he wondered. Now, wide awake, aware of what had actually taken place between them, what thoughts were going through her mind? The idea of her hating him, detesting the very sight of him, caused a knot to twist in his gut. Tabor had become so important to him so quickly. If only there were something he could say to her to right the wrong. Their lovemaking had been sensational, but it should never have happened under the circumstances. Still, his little voice told him that if he turned back the clock, he'd do it all again because he'd be unable to stop himself.

He sighed and walked over to the bar. "Drink?" he asked, his back to her.

"No, thank you," she said quietly. Oh, great, she thought, glancing at him. Jared looked as gorgeous in jeans as he did in a tuxedo. He didn't play fair.

Jared poured himself a drink, decided he didn't want it, and turned to face her. She met his gaze steadily, but he couldn't decipher the expression on her face.

"Are you all right?" he asked.

"Yes."

"I don't know what to say to you, Tabor."

"You've made your feelings clear," she said. He was sorry they'd made love. Oh, dear heaven, how that hurt. It didn't matter to him that she had no regrets; *he* wished it had never happened. He'd lost control and succumbed to . . . what? Pure male lust? And now he was uncomfortable in her presence because Jared Loring was a man of control and he'd just lost his control with her. He'd admitted that their lovemaking had been beautiful, special to him, yet it meant nothing to him. *She* meant nothing to him. Damn the man. "I suggest you forget what happened, Jared." *She* never would. And *she* would never regret it.

Forget? Jared thought dryly. Hell, he wanted to carry her back to bed and make love to her for the next twenty-four hours straight. "Is that what you plan to do? Forget it ever happened?"

"Is it necessary to continue talking about this? I told you I had no regrets, you obviously do, and we're poles apart on the subject."

Jared sat down in a chair. "You'll have regrets once you really think it through."

"Are you in the habit of making up people's minds for them, or am I a unique case? I'm a grown woman, Jared Loring. I don't need you to tell me how I feel, what I'm thinking, what my reactions are. I'm perfectly capable of figuring all that out on my own. But don't worry, I won't bother you with my opinion on this matter again. You've decided how it is, and that's that." She paused. "I believe you wanted to ask me something about Finn?"

Jared narrowed his eyes as he studied her. Dammit, he thought, she was really confusing him. He couldn't read her at all. Why wasn't she crying, or throwing things at him, or calling him a slew of rotten names? What was she feeling? Well, one thing was becoming very clear. He sure as hell didn't understand women very well, and he was beginning to think he didn't understand Tabor O'Casey at all.

"Jared? What about Finn? Have you found out anything?"

"What? Oh, yes, we've got some information. Tabor, your father obtained an incriminating list of some very important people involved in gun running. The list was stolen by Cat from a man called Mickey Mason."

"I've heard of him. He's a dangerous, ruthless man involved in hideous things. He's never spent a day in prison because he's clever and has the money to buy off the people he needs."

"True. When Finn realized a trap had been set, he called you to say he was coming home. Sometime between that call and when he would have arrived, Mason's boys picked him up."

Tabor clutched her hands tightly in her lap. "I see."

"But Finn managed to switch the contents of the bag before they got him. There were pages from a telephone book in it."

She gasped. "You're kidding. Then Finn must still be alive because he's the only one who knows where the list is."

"That's what we're hoping."

"But, Jared, Mickey Mason will—will demand that Finn tell him where the list is. He must have muscle on his payroll who will . . ." The color drained from her face. "Oh, God."

"Take it easy, okay?" Jared said gently. He wanted to go to her and hold her, tell her everything was going to be fine. But he couldn't touch her, not ever again. "The Mouse needs Finn alive and healthy." He leaned forward. "Tabor, if Finn refuses to talk, Mason may decide he should try another approach. You."

"Me? I don't know where the list is."

"No, but if Finn thought you were in danger, he'd probably talk to protect you. It's extremely important that you don't leave this suite. I can keep you safe here." From everyone except himself.

Safe from thugs with guns, Tabor thought. But who would shield her from the emotions Jared aroused in her? Who was going to keep her heart from being shattered into a million pieces if her affection for this man went any deeper?

"Tabor, I want you to think very carefully about that phone call Finn made to you. Was there any noise in the background to give a clue as to where he was? Mason's boys weren't far behind Finn, and there were pages from a telephone book in the bag. I think the list is close by the phone he used to call you. Did you hear anything?"

"Yes," Tabor said slowly, searching her mind. "Yes, I did hear something. I didn't think about it until now because I was so worried about Finn, and trying to pay close attention to what he was saying to me."

"What did you hear?"

"A name. A woman saying a name. Jared, it was a paging system, I'm sure of it. I honestly forgot about it, but, yes, it was a woman's voice paging a—a doctor."

"Doctor?"

"Yes. She said . . . She said, 'Dr. Rosengren to Emergency, please. Dr. Simon Rosengren to Emergency.' "

"You're beautiful," Jared said, striding to the telephone. He snatched up the receiver and punched Turtle's number.

"Mrs. Tuttle."

"It's Jared. Get on the phone to California. Find out which hospital has a doctor named Simon Rosengren on its staff. Start with the area between Beverly Hills and the north shore docks."

"Got it, General MacArthur."

"Would you knock off that general stuff?"

"You're so cute when you're angry. I'll get back to you soon. Ta-ta."

Jared replaced the receiver and began to pace the floor. "Okay," he said, finally stopping to look at Tabor again. "So far it fits. Finn went into a hospital because he knew it would be well lit, and Mouse's boys would have to wait for him to come out. But—" He stared up at the ceiling for a long moment.

"But?" she prompted.

"He told you he was on his way home, right?"

"Yes. He said we'd decide what to do next."

Jared shook his head. "No, he knew he didn't stand much chance getting past those men. That's why he switched the list in the hospital and tore pages from the telephone book in the booth he was in. It wouldn't take much to snap off the lock on the bag. He didn't want you to fall apart at that point, and he knew exactly what you'd do when he didn't arrive home."

"Come to you. Finn knew I'd come to you."

Jared nodded. "Your brother is Cat O'Casey's son all right. He bought time. He'll hold out against Mason as long as he can, then say he managed to get the list to you through a friend at the hospital, or he mailed it from there, whatever. Then, acting as though he's giving up and can't take any more, he'll tell Mason that you had instructions to come to me if there was ever any trouble. Finn knows that by now you're safely under wraps. He's leaving the rest to me."

She stood up. It was her turn to pace. "But, Jared, he didn't tell me where the list was so we could bargain with it. He doesn't want us to trade the list for him, does he? He's taking the chance that you can free him and the list will go to the proper people like my father wanted."

"Yes," he said quietly, "that's the way I see it."

"Oh, dear God. Finn is risking his life to carry out my father's final wishes. Finn knows I'm safe here with you and he's . . . oh, Jared, my brother . . ."

"Hey, easy," Jared said, closing the distance between them. He lifted one hand, then dropped it back to his side, not touching her. "We're putting the pieces together. I think we'll hear from Mason very soon."

Tabor wrapped her arms around herself in a protective gesture. "They're hurting him, aren't they? They're hurting Finn." A shudder ripped through her.

"Tabor, don't." He hesitated for a moment, then drew her into his embrace. She released her tight grip on herself and slid her arms around his back, leaning her head on his chest. "Don't do this to yourself, Tabor. I can feel you trembling. You said that Finn is a strong man in good condition. Besides that, he's smart, very smart. He's come through like a pro so far."

"He's not a pro, he's an artist. He's gentle and sensitive and . . . well, he did punch out a few guys who pestered me while we were growing up."

"Even artists have their moments," Jared said, inhaling the sweet fragrance of her hair.

She sighed, and he groaned inwardly as her breasts pressed more firmly against his chest. Heat surged through him, and in his mind's eye he saw her naked in his bed, her skin glowing in the soft light. He saw her lift her arms to him, welcoming him. And he saw the expression on her face when he brought her to fulfillment.

They had been incredible together, he thought, perfectly matched, sharing equally. If only he hadn't seduced her while she was hazy with sleep. She'd been dreaming of him, and he knew that when she'd first opened her eyes and spoken to him she thought it was all a dream. He, scum that he was, had played on that, used it to his own advantage. He'd lost control and satisfied his own selfish desire.

But he wanted her again, now, that very minute . . . and forever.

Forever? he repeated in his mind. Forever was not a word he associated with women. Forever was commitment, forsaking all those delectable others.

Forever was love, and love was not in the cards for Jared Loring. He had no desire whatsoever to be turned into a blithering, starry-eyed idiot by a woman. Love was fine for those who didn't mind having their buttons pushed by another person, but not for Jared Loring. No way.

Tabor nestled closer to him, and he tightened his hold on her, gritting his teeth against the torturous heat rocketing through him. He could feel her relax, the tension and fear ebbing from her slender body. He forced his hands to be still, not to tangle in her enticing hair, not to roam over her luscious curves.

It was suddenly very important to him, he realized, that Tabor know she was safe in his arms, protected not only from others who wished to harm her but from himself. He hated the idea that she might ever cringe from his touch in fear that seduction would follow. He had to know that she trusted him, not only in regard to her brother, but in every aspect of her life.

Why did it matter so much to him what Tabor thought, he wondered. Yes, he was feeling guilty as hell about what had happened in his bed. But he was also confused about that because he had yet to understand Tabor's attitude toward it all. Maybe she was going to have a delayed reaction and would still end up punching him in the nose.

Women were so damn complicated. And Tabor O'Casey was by far the most complex woman he'd ever met. Thank the Lord that he was not susceptible to falling in love, because Tabor was capable of throwing him way off kilter. But he knew that now, and was back in control.

Tabor lifted her head to meet his gaze. "Thank you, Jared," she said softly. "I was suddenly so frightened for Finn, and as Cat used to say, I needed a warm hug. You're very kind, and I do thank you."

He dropped his arms from her and stepped back, swearing so fiercely that her eyes widened in surprise. He glared at her, and she matched his expression, her hands planted on her hips.

"Oh, yes, I forgot," she said. "I'm not allowed to express my gratitude to you for anything, am I? I can't say thank you or tell you how much I appreciate all that you've done and have yet to do for me and for Finn. And heaven forbid I should discuss our lovemaking, because you've already made up your mind that it was a giant mistake."

"Look, Tabor—"

"No, you look, Jared Loring. You keep yourself removed from people, not letting anyone get too close, moving inside your very carefully protected space. Don't you get lonely in there, Jared? How can the sunshine warm you through those walls? Well, I'll tell you this. If you refuse to acknowledge our lovemaking for the beautiful experience it was, then it's your loss. I will cherish what we shared, treasure the memories of it."

"Tabor—"

"Quiet. I agreed to follow your orders, do as I'm

told in regard to this horrifying situation with Finn. But I will not be told what I'm feeling as a woman. This may be hard for you to fathom, buster, but there are certain areas of life that are not under your command. And my emotions are one of them." She spun around and marched into the bedroom.

Jared blinked. Buster? Lord, Tabor was mad as hell. One minute she was shaking with fear in his arms, and then the next she was telling him where he could put himself. Where did she get off asking him if he was lonely? Of course he wasn't lonely. His life was set up exactly the way he wanted it. As for having enough sunshine to warm him, he . . . Hell, he wasn't taking the time to think about this stuff.

He glowered at the bedroom door, then a slow smile tugged his lips and he shook his head. Tabor was really something, he mused. She was just as beautiful when angry as she was when glowing with passion. She was even beautiful when she cried. And she was beautiful when she was sleeping, and . . .

"Oh, Loring, can it," he said in disgust.

The telephone rang and he strode across the room to snatch up the receiver.

"Loring."

"Mrs. Tuttle here, y'all. I am reportin' in to you, sweet potato, on that little ol' info y'all wanted."

"How nice," Jared said, rolling his eyes. "And what, pray tell, has brought on your rendition of Scarlett O'Hara?"

"I figure y'all must get homesick for the South, honey pie. Seeing how I'm your substitute granny, I thought I'd bring y'all a touch of home."

"You're weird, Turtle."

"I'm lovable, Rhett. I also have the name of the hospital where your doc is. What's it worth to you?"

"Ah, I see. You're in the mood to dicker."

"We Yankees don't give in easy to you Southern boys. What's your offer, O mighty master of the plantation?"

"Try this on for size. You're coming out of retirement for one assignment. One, Turtle. Make sure you get that part clear."

"Hot diggity damn! A disguise, the whole bit?"

"Yep."

"Sold. What am I going to be?"

"A nurse."

"Boring, but I'll grab it. Hey, do I get to fly to the coast in your private plane? I assume I'm going to this hospital that I found."

"Yes, you can fly in the private plane. No, you may not touch any of the controls or even go into the cockpit."

"Damn."

"Can't win them all. Get Sylvia to cover for you on the phone, then meet me in the small office downstairs with Trig and I'll fill you in. You can catch some sleep on the plane. Call the airport and our pilot so that the plane is ready to go. I'll be down in about fifteen minutes."

"Gotcha. Why can't I be a doctor instead of a nurse?"

"A nurse. Take it or leave it."

"I'll take it. Is Trig going with me?"

"Yes. This could be sticky, Turtle. I'd go myself, but I need to be here in case I'm contacted, and also to protect Tabor."

"Trig said the Mouse has Tabor's brother."

"Yeah, he does."

"Mouse is bad news, Jared."

"I know. Believe me, Turtle, I know."

"Well, we'll just have to get Cat O'Casey's boy out of Mouse's grimy paws."

"That's the plan."

"I'm leaping into action, Rhett."

"Don't leap, Turtle, you'll break something. I'll see you downstairs."

"Okeydokey."

Jared replaced the receiver, then walked slowly to the bedroom door. He leaned his shoulder against the doorjamb and gazed at Tabor where she lay in bed, the blankets pulled up to her throat.

"You heard?" he asked quietly.

She turned her head to meet his gaze. "Yes. Everyone is being so wonderful, so willing to help." She paused. "Jared, I apologize for my outburst. It was uncalled for and not even true. It's obvious from what I've seen here at Miracles that you do care about people, let them get close to you. It's as though you're the head of a wonderfully loyal family. I guess . . . I don't know . . . maybe I feel like an outsider, watching from the sidelines. Anyway, I hope you'll accept my apology for screaming at you like that."

He walked into the room and sat down in the chair he'd placed next to the bed earlier.

"Oh, Tabor," he said with a sigh, "*you're* apologizing to *me*? After what I did?"

"Jared, please, don't, not again. Don't keep denigrating what we shared. I wanted you, I wanted to make love with you. Why is that so hard for you to accept? Because you lost control of the situation? Does it matter, really matter? I suppose if I ask you what you're afraid of, you'll fly into a rage."

He smiled. "Probably."

"You're a complicated man, Jared Loring."

"I was just thinking that you're a complicated woman."

She laughed. "Well, at least we agree on something." Her smile faded. "I just wish . . . well, never mind."

He picked up her hand and held it between both of his, staring at her delicate fingers for a long moment before meeting her gaze again.

"I really believe," he said softly, "that you should be very angry about what happened between us. But you're right, I can't tell you how to feel about things, what your emotions should be. You're a woman who knows her own mind, and I respect that. You keep telling me that you have no regrets about what we shared. All right, Tabor, I'll accept and respect that too."

"But *you* regret it. You're sorry it ever took place."

"No man could regret something so incredibly beautiful, so very special. I wanted you, Tabor, from the first moment I saw you. What I can't handle is losing control, feeling that I seduced you when you weren't aware of what you were doing. I'm angry at myself, and I've told myself I mustn't touch you again."

"Don't I have a voice in that decision?"

He placed her hand back on the blanket and stood, then leaned down to brush his lips over hers.

"No," he said, his mouth close to hers. "I've lost control once with you. I won't run the risk of it happening again. I can't deal with that." He straightened. "Get some sleep. I have to go meet with Turtle and Trig." He turned and walked from the room.

"Add stubborn to complicated," Tabor said to the empty room.

She shut off the light and closed her eyes, and her thoughts turned immediately to Finn, to what might be happening to him. When she slept, she was plagued by haunting nightmares.

When Tabor awakened, she glanced at the clock on the nightstand and saw that it was after ten. She'd just about slept the morning away, she realized, and despite her disturbing dreams felt well rested.

She turned her head on the pillow and nearly gasped aloud. Clad only in jeans and sleeping soundly next to her was Jared Loring. He lay on top of the bedspread, one hand resting on his bare chest, the other on the bed.

She sat up and gazed at him. Even in sleep his power and strength were there. He was a man's man, born with a self-confidence and sense of authority that others could only envy. And he was a woman's man. His body, his face, were close to perfection, his unusual silver hair adding to his rugged appeal. His blatant masculinity made a woman acutely aware of her own femininity, of being the counterpart to this incredible man. There were so many facets to Jared. Tough, aloof, quick to anger, caring, warm, tender. The list went on.

He was, Tabor knew, a man of the night and of control, a man who lived alone, following the rigid rules he'd dictated to himself. Being in love with Jared would not be a smooth road of bliss. But, oh, it would be glorious if he lowered those walls and returned that love. He would love with the same intensity with which he lived.

Was she falling in love with Jared Loring, Tabor wondered. She didn't know, and she wouldn't begin to sort through all her inner turmoil now. There was Finn to think of, and her fears for him never left her for very long. Later she'd get in touch with herself and examine the new and sometimes frightening emotions Jared had planted in her.

Her gaze skimmed over his entire body as she remembered the ecstasy of their lovemaking. Jared was so angry for losing control, and for, he was convinced, seducing her. She'd gotten him to accept that she wasn't sorry about their lovemaking, but he refused to lessen the anger directed at himself. And because of that anger he would never make love to her again.

A wave of icy misery swept through Tabor, and although she was so close to Jared, she felt lonely and alone. He was building the walls around him even higher and stronger, determined to keep her at a distance. Yet, he had said their lovemaking had been beautiful and very special. Didn't he want to go further, she wondered, to discover *why* it had been so special, *why* they had been attracted to each other from the outset? Didn't he wish to know what this was between them that was growing more intense with every passing hour?

Well, she thought decisively, maybe Jared was capable of slamming the doors on his emotions, but she was not. She had to know what her true feelings for Jared Loring were.

Even if it meant discovering she was in love with him.

Even if it meant having her heart broken because he could never love her in return.

She had to know, and in order to know, she had to get beyond Jared's walls.

She pondered what she could do, then had an idea. What if she showed Jared that he hadn't seduced her, hadn't done anything she wouldn't willingly agree to again? Oh, heavens, did she have the courage to do this? The man was dead to the world and she was contemplating . . . yes, she could do it because there was a chance it might weaken the walls surrounding him.

Wishing her heart weren't beating so wildly, Tabor slid from beneath the blankets and slowly, carefully, stretched out next to Jared. She wiggled closer, watching for any sign that he might be awakening. He slept on.

The next part, she knew, was going to be tricky. Jared had been an agent for years, and would still possess razor-sharp reflexes and fine-tuned senses. If she found herself being tossed across the room, she'd definitely know she'd done a lousy job.

Okay, Tabor, she told herself, go for it.

She moved up and onto his hard body. He jerked in surprise and opened his eyes, only inches from hers.

"What—" he started.

"Shh," she said, and covered his lips with hers.

She felt his muscles tense beneath her, and he refused to open his mouth despite the insistent pressure of her tongue. This was not going well, she thought frantically. She'd never tried to seduce a man in her life, and she obviously wasn't going to graduate at the top of her class if Jared didn't cooperate, the rat.

She flicked her tongue over his tightly closed mouth, back and forth, slowly, sensually, matching the rhythm of the sway of her breasts on his chest and her hips on his. At last he groaned and parted his lips, and her tongue slipped into his mouth. His arms came up to embrace her, one hand on her buttocks, pressing her more firmly into the cradle of his hips. His arousal was heavy against her, and she purred as she explored every crevice of his mouth. He moaned. The kiss intensified into a frantic, frenzied meeting of lips and tongues.

In the next instant Tabor was flipped onto her back and covered by the heavy weight of Jared, who stared down at her with a stormy expression on his face.

"What in the hell do you think you're doing?"

"You cheat," she said breathlessly. "I was up there, and you were down here. Put me back."

"No. Answer the question."

"You're crushing me."

"I am not. Now, answer the question."

"I was proving a point, but you screwed it up. No. Wrong. Bad choice of words. You deviated from my plan."

"Plan," he repeated. "This ought to be good. And what, Miss O'Casey, was your plan?"

"Well, I was reenacting what you consider to be the crime, only this time *you* were asleep and *I* was awake. Get it?"

"No."

"Oh. You obviously were aware of what you were doing and what I was doing to you once you were fully awake. I was not seducing you then, Jared, any more than you seduced me when we made love. I had a choice, you would have had a choice. I just . . . I just wanted you to let go of the anger you're directing at yourself. It's so unnecessary, and I thought if I could prove that to you . . . oh, I feel like an idiot. I think this is where I say 'It seemed like a good idea at the time.' Get off me and go back to sleep."

"No."

"Then get off me and don't go back to sleep."

"No."

"Jared, move your body."

"No."

"Why not?"

"Because I'm thinking. I did lose control of myself when I woke you, Tabor."

"But I didn't. I wanted you, Jared, don't you see? If I hadn't wanted you, if I had said no, you would have stopped. You wouldn't have forced yourself on me. You may think you lost control, but all you were doing was taking what was being offered openly, honestly, willingly. It was so wonderful between us. Don't tarnish it with misplaced anger at yourself."

"Why does how I feel about it matter so much to you?"

"I don't know, I really don't. Maybe a part of me is afraid you're sorry you made love to me at all, no matter what the circumstances might have been."

"No, oh, Tabor, no. I wanted you. I've never wanted

any woman the way I did you, the way I do right now, as I'm sure you can feel."

"I'm wide awake," she whispered, "and so are you. I want you to make love with me, Jared, but the choice is yours. I don't want there to be any doubt in your mind that you're in complete control of what you're doing. It's too important."

"You're an incredible woman, Tabor O'Casey. I've never met anyone like you before, and I have no idea what to do about you. Except at the moment. I'm going to make love to you. Wide awake, no regrets . . . this is ours. We'll worry about the future later." He lowered his head toward hers. "Much later."

Their lovemaking was slow and sweet, as though there were no world beyond that room, no people other than the two of them. They touched, kissed, and explored as if they had both just discovered a rare and wondrous treasure. Hands and lips missed no inch of the other's body. They gave and took and shared equally.

When at last their passions were at a fever pitch and they could bear no more, they became one, their pounding rhythm perfectly matched. Just one heartbeat apart they were hurled into the ultimate oblivion, clinging and calling out to each other. Slowly, reluctantly, they returned to reality. Jared moved off Tabor and circled her waist with his arm, his lips resting lightly on her forehead.

"Wonderful," she said softly.

"Very."

"No regrets."

"No, no regrets, Tabor. But—"

"But what?"

"No promises either. No commitments or . . . I

have to be honest with you because I don't want to hurt you. I move through life alone, I always have. It's only fair that you know that."

So, Tabor thought, this was how it felt to love a man who didn't love her. To suffer this cold pain. She knew now she was in love with Jared Loring. And Jared Loring was making it very clear that he was never going to fall in love with her.

"I understand," she said, her voice hoarse as she blinked back her tears. "Don't worry, Jared, I understand."

Five

For the remainder of the morning and on into the afternoon time crept by slowly for Tabor. Still holding her tightly in his arms, Jared had fallen asleep. She'd stayed there, her hand resting on his chest to feel the steady beat of his heart. She'd studied his handsome face, memorizing it so that in the years ahead she would see him clearly in her mind.

She knew her father would say she'd chosen well in picking Jared Loring to give her heart to. Cat had admired and respected Jared for many years. But Cat had known Jared only on a man-to-man level, and wouldn't think of him as someone who would never commit himself to one woman for all time. A man who would never fall in love. Jared had been completely honest with her, and she should be grateful for that, but it did nothing to ease the ache in her heart.

Eventually she slipped from his embrace, managing not to wake him. After showering and dressing in brown pleated slacks and a yellow silk blouse, she called room service and had lunch sent up.

The hours ticked by slowly. Her mind bounced back and forth between Jared and Finn, torturing her with vivid pictures of the two most important men in her life. No one came to Jared's suite, no one telephoned. All was quiet. Tabor felt as though every other person on earth had forgotten and deserted her.

She often stood at the window to watch the people stroll along the sidewalk, the cars inch ahead in the heavy traffic, assuring herself that there was a normal world beyond her bubble of isolation. When memories of her lovemaking with Jared flooded her mind, a soft smile would touch her lips, and she could feel a warm flush on her cheeks that accompanied the simmering heat of desire deep within her.

How glorious they were together, she mused, how perfectly matched. Already she felt she knew every inch of his body, and delighted in learning what gave him the greatest pleasure and heightened his passion. They gave and received equally, and when they became one, it was as though the intimate act had been created just for them.

But on the heels of those memories was the harsh reminder that she had fallen in love with a man who would never return that love. She refused to cry, and held the tears inside like a cold block of ice that seemed to grow heavier as the hours passed.

In the middle of the afternoon she nearly sobbed aloud with relief when she heard the shower running. Jared was awake. Thank heavens she would at last have someone to talk to, something other than the taunting voices in her mind to listen to.

The shower stopped and she stared at the closed bedroom door. She was suddenly nervous, and told herself it was ridiculous. Jared was beyond that door, not a stranger. But she was afraid that he might see, might somehow sense the change in her, know by looking at her that she had fallen irrevocably in love with him. No, no, no, she mustn't give a clue to her true feelings, or her pride would be shattered along with her heart. Jared Loring would never know that Tabor O'Casey loved him.

The bedroom door opened. Tabor's heartbeat raced as Jared walked into the room. He was wearing gray slacks and a black dress shirt open at the neck, the clothes accentuating his bronze skin and silver hair. He crossed the room to her and framed her face in his hands.

"Hello, beautiful Tabor," he said, his voice low and husky.

"Hello," she managed to whisper.

His mouth melted over hers, and she responded instantly. Forgotten were the long, agonizing hours spent alone. Forgotten was the chill within her as the ice melted under the rising heat of her passion. Forgotten was everything but the taste, the feel, the aroma, of Jared.

She leaned into him, her hands splayed on his back, savoring him, wanting him, loving him. He met her tongue with his own, his hands tangling in her luxurious hair. His manhood surged, evidence once again of his want of her, his burning need.

At last he lifted his head. "I didn't mean to sleep this long, but if I don't stop kissing you, we're going to end up right back in that bed." He dropped his hands and stepped away. "You are so beautiful, Tabor."

"So are you," she said, her voice unsteady.

He chuckled softly, then turned and walked to the telephone. "Have you eaten?"

"Yes."

"I need some food." He placed an order, then called Turtle.

"Mrs. Tuttle."

"Florence Nightingale, I presume?" he said.

"Don't speak to me, Jared Loring. Don't you say one syrupy-sweet Southern word to me."

"Good Lord, what is your problem? Bad flight? The pilot followed my orders and wouldn't let you fly the plane? What?"

"Talk to Trig. He's been waiting to hear that you're awake. I'll tell him to come up there. Be prepared to be strangled by my bare hands when I see you. Oh, I'm so furious I could spit." She hung up with a thud.

Jared frowned, staring at the receiver for a moment before replacing it. "Something must have gone wrong. Turtle is ready to shoot me on sight."

"Wrong?" Tabor asked. "About Finn?"

"Trig will be up in a minute to report. We'll know then."

"Jared, nothing is happening. I'm so worried about Finn. Why haven't we heard anything?"

"I don't know, Tabor. Let's see what Trig has to say."

"Yes, all right. I'm sorry. It's been a long day."

"I shouldn't have left you alone for so long." He smiled at her. "It would seem that a certain Miss O'Casey just wore me out."

America's most popular, most compelling romance novels...

Here, at last...love stories that really involve you!
Fresh, finely crafted novels with story lines so
believable you'll feel you're actually living them!
Characters you can relate to...exciting places to
visit...unexpected plot twists...all in all, exciting
romances that satisfy your mind and delight
your heart.

- -

EXAMINE 6
LOVESWEPT NOVELS FOR
15 Days FREE!

To introduce you to this fabulous service, you'll get six brand-new
Loveswept releases not yet in the bookstores. These six exciting new
titles are yours to examine for 15 days without obligation to buy. Keep
them if you wish for just $12.50 plus postage and handling and any
applicable sales tax. Offer available in U.S.A. only.

☐ **YES,** please send me six new romances for a 15-day
FREE examination. If I keep them, I will pay just $12.50 (that's six
books for the price of five) plus postage and handling and any
applicable sales tax and you will enter my name on your preferred
customer list to receive all six new Loveswept novels published each
month *before* they are released to the bookstores—always on the
same 15-day free examination basis.

40311

Name_____

Address_____

City_____

State_____ Zip_____

My Guarantee: I am never required to buy any shipment unless I
wish. I may preview each shipment for 15 days. If I don't want it, I
simply return the shipment within 15 days and owe nothing for it.

"Oh, hush," she said, feeling once again the warm flush on her cheeks.

There was a knock on the door, and the screen above showed Trig with a serving cart. Jared opened the door.

"Come in, Trig. Hello, Joe."

"Mr. Loring," the huge man guarding the door said.

"Howdy, boss," Trig said, whipping the cart into the room. "Hi, Tabor."

"Hello, Trig."

"Want some of this, Tabor?" Jared asked, gesturing toward the dishes on the cart.

"No, thank you," she said, sitting on the sofa.

Jared pulled a chair up to the table and sat down. "Okay, Trig, sit. Fill me in on what happened in California. Why is Turtle so damn mad?"

Trig slouched into one of the easy chairs. "Turtle is fuming, boss, because it was so easy it was practically over before it started. She was all decked out in one of them spiffy nurse's outfits, even had shoes that sounded like wet sponges when she walked."

"And?" Jared asked. He popped a French fry into his mouth.

"The pay phones were in the lobby of the hospital. No one was looking at us, and we just strolled from one to the next. Finn had stuck the list under one of the ledges with—ready?—chewing gum." He pulled some papers from his pocket. "There you go, boss. The list. We were in and out in ten minutes. Lordy, Turtle is hot. She got all dressed up for nothing. I think she thought she was going to get to perform brain surgery or something."

Jared laughed, then sobered as he unfolded the

papers and looked at them. "Holy—" He whistled as he read some of the names. "Mason is going to make enemies in high places if these guys are picked up."

"No joke," Trig said. "I peeked at the list. The Mouse won't be able to run fast enough or far enough to escape from those yo-yo's. He needs that list back real bad, boss. The man will be ready to do business with you."

"But when?" Tabor asked. "What's taking so long?"

"Finn is playing it safe, Tabor," Jared said. "He's making sure his story holds up. There has to have been time for the list to reach you somehow, then you had to get here."

"I'd say we'll hear from Mickey anytime now," Trig said. "Wouldn't you, boss?"

Jared nodded. "Yes. Trig, tell Splice to put tracing devices on my phones up here in the suite and the office, and on the one in the small office downstairs."

"Right," Trig said, getting to his feet.

"Nice job, Trig," Jared added, looking at the list again. "Tell Turtle she did fine."

"I'm not going near Turtle until she cools off."

"I'm not either. Is Nick on the floor?"

"Yeah, he's down there. He's charming the socks off a busload of little old ladies from a retirement home."

"Okay."

"Thank you, Trig," Tabor said.

"Hey, you bet. I love flying in that jazzy plane. Coming back with a crabby Turtle wasn't wonderful though. We've got the edge, Tabor. You'll be with your brother real soon, you'll see. 'Bye for now, folks." He left the suite.

"Now what?" Tabor asked Jared.

"I put the list in the safe and we wait."

She moaned. "I'm going crazy waiting."

"I know it's difficult, Tabor. Look, you must be getting cabin fever in here. I'll take you down on the floor tonight, okay? Providing, of course, we don't hear from Mason in the meantime. Yes, that's a good idea. If anyone is watching, word will get back to him that you're here. We'll go down about eight. In the meantime I'll finish my lunch, then we'll watch a movie. Why don't you go over to the bookcase and decide which one you want to see?"

"You don't have to baby-sit me, Jared."

"I want to be with you. I'm going to tuck you close to my side and keep you there."

For how long, Tabor asked silently as she crossed the room. Just during the movie? Until Finn was safely returned? How long would Jared want to be with her, have her by his side? Their time together was being determined by other events. Once this was all finished, then what? Would Jared say it had been great, kiss her good-bye, and get on with his life and forget her? Was that how easy it was for him to move from one woman to the next?

Jared continued to eat as he watched Tabor inspect the movie cassettes. She looked good in this room, he thought. It suited her. And Lord knew she looked good, felt good, was good, in his bed. Their lovemaking . . . no, he'd better not dwell on it, or he'd be dragging her back into the bedroom instead of watching a movie.

No commitments, no promises, he reminded himself. He'd told her that so she wouldn't be hurt, but even as he had said the words, a sharp pain had stabbed him. A picture of her leaving him, picking up her suitcase and walking out the door, had flashed through his mind. He'd lost count of the women who'd walked out that door, couldn't remember all of their faces or names. But the thought of Tabor leaving . . .

"Forget it," he said softly, getting to his feet. Of course she was leaving. When this mess with Mason was squared away, she'd go back to California, her business, her own life. He'd never see her again.

He stared at her as she read a blurb on the back of a cassette. He'd never see her again, he repeated to himself. Never hold her, touch her, make love to her. Never hear her laugh, see her smile. She would be gone, and he would be alone. And lonely? Would she take his sunshine when she went? Damn, these thoughts were crazy, weren't like him at all. But then, he'd been off kilter from the moment he'd seen Tabor. He wished to heaven he understood what this woman was doing to him.

He grabbed the list and locked it in the safe in his bedroom. When he returned to the living room, he called Turtle.

"Mrs. Tuttle."

"Before you blow a fuse, listen," he said.

"Humph."

"Humph? Nobody says that."

"I do," Turtle said. "Humph."

He sighed. "Listen, Turtle, we go to Code Dark Blue at seven tonight. Tabor and I will be down on the floor at eight."

"Code Dark Blue? My darling boy, I have just forgiven you all your sins."

He laughed. "You're a sweetheart, sweetheart. Tell Nick to grab a nap now because I'll want him to be around tonight. Have him arrange work schedules first, then sack out. I'll be up here with Tabor if anyone needs me. Have Chuck cover the floor."

"Gotcha. I love ya, cutie pie."

"You're a fickle woman, Turtle."

"The name is Mrs. Tuttle, Mr. Loring. I'm a key figure in the Code Dark Blue team, so watch your mouth. Show a little respect."

"Yes, ma'am. Good-bye, ma'am." He hung up. "Poor thing, she's nuts."

Tabor laughed, and Jared turned to look at her. She was smiling at him from across the room, then another burst of laughter escaped from her lips and danced through the air.

He walked slowly toward her. "Are you going to let me in on what's so funny?" he asked.

"You're wonderful," she said, still smiling. "You're so good with people, Jared. You understand those who are close to you, and you know how to make them feel special and important. You treat everyone as an individual, not to manipulate them, but because you care, really care."

A dark flush crept up his neck and along his cheekbones. "I—um, I think I'll pass on commenting on that. Did you find a movie you want to see?"

Jared was blushing! Tabor thought incredulously. Tough guy Jared Loring was blushing because he didn't know what to do with a compliment directed to the very warm, human side of him. Oh, how she loved this complicated man. He was all and everything she'd ever hoped and dreamed she'd find in a man. He was capable of such deep love. If only he loved her.

"Tabor, do you want to watch a movie or not?"

"What? Oh, yes, I do. Here."

She handed him a cassette and he looked at the title. "*Star Trek III*?"

She sat down on the sofa, facing the big screen. "Absolutely. I'm ready, Admiral, for a voyage on the starship *Enterprise*. I'm prepared to go where no man has gone before."

He chuckled. "Okay. We're off to scout outer space, my dear."

He started the movie and settled next to her on the sofa, and Tabor instantly knew she would never be able to concentrate on the plot. She was just so incredibly aware of Jared, every magnificent, muscled inch of him. And she was acutely aware of herself as well. His woman, for as long as she was with him.

This movie was one of Jared's favorites, but how in the hell was he supposed to concentrate with Tabor sitting so close to him? She smelled like flowers. Her hair was brushing over his arm. He couldn't stop staring at her breasts, soft and full beneath her silk blouse. If she turned her head right now while he was looking at her, he could capture her mouth with his.

She slowly turned her head to meet his gaze.

"Thank you," he murmured, and kissed her before he could tell himself that had been a dumb thing to say.

"Warp factor eight," came the voice from the screen.

Amen to that, Jared thought, and thrust his tongue deep into her mouth.

She was necking at the movies, Tabor thought giddily, wrapping her arms around Jared's back.

The kiss was long and powerful, and their breathing was ragged when Jared finally lifted his head. He cleared his throat, resisted the urge to kiss Tabor again, and directed his attention to the screen.

"Watch the movie," he said gruffly. "There will be a test on it later to see if you grasped the social statement being made."

Tabor laughed, and Jared joined her, smiling at her warmly.

For the remainder of the film they loudly cheered on the good guys, booed the villains, shouted warnings when danger approached, and applauded when all went well. They had a wonderful time.

Tabor felt a twinge of guilt when she thought of Finn, but then somehow knew her brother would approve of her actions. Not just watching a movie, but also making love with Jared. And she also realized Finn would not accept her fatalistic attitude that she was destined to leave Las Vegas with a broken heart because the man she loved did not love her.

Do something about it, Finn would say. But what, she wondered. She was no femme fatale, didn't know the art of twisting men around her little finger, especially a man like Jared. No, if he was to come to love her, it would be Jared Loring falling in love with Tabor O'Casey just as she was. Right now it appeared that getting her heart broken was guaranteed.

For dinner they feasted on exquisite poached salmon, and afterward settled on the sofa to enjoy snifters of brandy.

"Do you have a really fancy dress with you?" Jared asked.

"Just the one I was wearing when I snuck in here."

"I think you should wear a knockout number when we go downstairs. Not that I think you'd go unnoticed in any crowd, you understand, but I want to make certain that Mason's boys see you if they're around."

"Where am I supposed to get this creation to wear?"

"I'll take care of it. I'll shower and change now, then go down to one of the boutiques here in the casino and have some dresses sent up for you to choose from. I'll be back for you later."

"You're going to pick out the dresses?"

He smiled. "Sure. I'll choose a few and you decide which one you like best."

"This ought to be interesting. I'm about to see Jared Loring's interpretation of a knockout number."

"Yes, ma'am," he said, getting to his feet. "You're in for a real treat."

"Had a lot of experience at this sort of thing, have you?"

"Darlin', you wound me. I'm just an innocent Southern boy."

She smiled sweetly. "Mr. Loring, that is a crock."

He laughed, bent over to give her a hard, fast kiss, then went into the bedroom, still smiling.

Oh, yes, Tabor thought, she truly did love that man.

Two hours later Tabor walked slowly around the bed, scrutinizing the four full-length gowns Jared had had delivered to the suite. He'd left earlier in his tuxedo, smelling of soap and aftershave, and looking gorgeous. Her heart had beat double-time for ten minutes after he'd kissed her very thoroughly and left.

She had showered, shampooed her hair, then blown it dry, brushing it until it shimmered. Clad only in a towel, she retraced her steps around the bed, still looking at the dresses.

Jared wanted knockout, and Jared would get knockout. There was no contest among the four creations.

She hung the other three dresses carefully in the closet, then picked up the one she had chosen and held it out in front of her.

"Without a doubt," she said decisively, "this will K.O. 'em."

Jared stepped out of the elevator and strode down the hall to his suite. He supposed he hadn't given Tabor enough time to get ready, but he'd been restless on the casino floor and had wanted her with him, close by his side.

That was because of Mason, he quickly told himself. It wasn't that he, Jared Loring, needed to have Tabor with him. It was the situation, the fact that he was tired of waiting for something to break loose about Finn. If Mason's men were skulking around to determine if Tabor O'Casey was, indeed, at Miracles, then Tabor had to be seen. *That* was why Jared had returned to his suite so soon.

"Good evening, Mr. Loring."

"Hello, Pico. I'm taking Tabor down to the casino for a while, but I'd like you to stay on duty here. If Tabor could get past my security system, so could someone else. She didn't quite make it, but she got farther than I would have thought possible. When things calm down, I'll have to take another look at our setup."

"Yes, sir. I'll stay right here."

Jared nodded, unlocked the door, and stepped into the suite. He saw Tabor instantly, and gaped at her.

"Hello, Jared," she said softly. "Do I pass inspection?"

His gaze skimmed over her, and heat surged throughout his body. The dress was red. It was a million glittering red sequins attached to material that lovingly hugged the curves of Tabor's body. One shoulder was entirely bare, the other draped with a narrow strip of the sequined fabric. Her hair was a shining golden waterfall tumbling down her back.

She was a vision of beauty, he thought hazily. Sensational. Stunning. His.

"You're beautiful, Tabor," he said huskily.

"You picked out the dress."

"It didn't look like that on the hanger."

She laughed, and Jared felt his body tighten even more.

"Do you think this will get the attention of Mickey's men if they're here?"

"Hell, every man in the place will be gawking at you. Are you positive that's the one you want to wear?"

"Oh, yes. I knew as soon as I saw it. You have excellent taste."

"I'm not so sure about that. Good Lord, Tabor, you're the most beautiful woman I've ever seen. I don't want every man downstairs mentally peeling that dress off you. I think you should change."

"No. I like this one."

"Wonderful," he said.

"Jared, you did pick it out, you know."

"Well, how in the hell was I supposed to realize you'd look like that in it?" He waved one hand in the air.

She shrugged. "You wanted knockout."

"I overdid it a bit," he said gruffly. "Go change."

"No." He cared, she thought dizzily. He was pouting, working up to a doozy of a tantrum because he didn't want any other men fantasizing about her. Jared was possessive of her—even, perhaps, jealous. He cared!

"Shall we go?" she asked, smiling pleasantly.

"No!" He sighed. "Yes. But stay right next to me, understand? If I have to stop and speak to someone, you stop. Don't wander off. Don't smile too much either. Act aloof."

"Oh, for Pete's sake," she said, laughing. "Why don't you just handcuff me to you?"

"Don't tempt me, lady. I swear to heaven that dress did not look like that on the hanger."

"I'm not built like a hanger."

"Believe me, Tabor, I'm very aware of that. Let's go."

"Certainly, sir." He cared, he cared, he cared, her heart echoed. Jared was in a lousy mood, and it was wonderful.

When he walked her past the elevator in the hall, she looked up at him questioningly. "Where are we going?"

"Might as well do it up right, I guess. You are going to make what is known as an entrance."

"Oh, how exciting."

Jared muttered an earthy expletive that Tabor ignored. They turned a corner, went down another long hallway, and were suddenly at the top of the sweeping staircase.

"Oh, Jared, it's fantastic. Just like Scarlett and Rhett."

He smiled at her and slipped her hand into the crook of his arm. "I had it specially made, a touch of Southern class and charm." His smile faded. "You are the most beautiful woman ever to walk down these stairs, Tabor. I guess that sounds corny, even phony, but I sincerely mean it."

"Thank you," she whispered, looking directly into his eyes.

They didn't move, or hardly breathe, for a long, heart-stopping moment, then Jared tore his gaze from Tabor's and they started down the stairs.

On the floor a dealer said, "Place your bets."

"Would you look at that?" one of the men at the table said.

"At what, sir?" the dealer asked. "You haven't placed your bet."

"The stairs. Take a gander at what's coming down those stairs."

The dealer's mouth fell open. No bets were placed at that table, or the one next to it, or the next three. All eyes were riveted on the stunning couple slowly descending the majestic staircase. Nick unhooked the velvet rope at the bottom, moving back with it to clear the way. Tabor and Jared stepped onto the casino floor and Nick put the rope into place.

"Good Lord," Nick muttered, staring at Tabor.

"Put your eyes back in your head, Capoletti," Jared said. He shot quick, dark glares at the dealers.

"Place your bets," one dealer nearly yelled.

The spell was broken and play resumed.

"Tabor," Nick said, "you look like a princess, or a movie star, or a—"

"Dammit, Nick," Jared said. "Quit gawking at her."

"I'm not gawking," Nick said, grinning. "I'm appreciating. There's probably a hundred guys in here who are gawking, but not me. We Italians have class. That is really some dress, Tabor."

She smiled. "Jared picked it out."

"Don't remind me," Jared said. "There's a lesson to be learned here, Nick. Women are not built like hangers."

"Huh?"

"Forget it. Anything going on down here that I should know about?"

"No," Nick said. "Do you really think Mickey the Mouse's big boys will show up here tonight?"

"I hope so. I've had it with this sitting around. I want to get this show on the road, then wrapped up and finished."

And then? Tabor wondered. Would she go home with her brother and be instantly forgotten by Jared?

She dipped her head for a moment in fear that the pain in her heart might be reflected in her eyes. When she lifted her head again, Nick was smiling at her. She forced a smile onto her lips, then to her amazement and confusion Nick winked at her.

For the next two hours Tabor, Jared, and Nick strolled through the casino, stopping often to allow Tabor to play at various tables with the chips Jared gave her. She lost consistently.

"You're an expensive date," Jared said, chuckling. "The object of blackjack, by the way, is to get as close as possible to twenty-one without going over, not see how high you can make your cards add up to."

Tabor shrugged. "Oh, well. I only lost little plastic chips."

"At five hundred smackers a pop," Nick said, laughing.

Her eyes widened. "You're kidding. Aren't you? Oh, Lord, you're not kidding. Jared, I'm so sorry. Why did you keep handing me those chips? I don't know how to play any of this stuff."

He laughed. "Don't worry about it. I have an inside track with the owner. I'll—" He stopped speaking as someone bumped his arm.

"Oh, excuse me, Mr. Loring," a cocktail waitress said. "I didn't see you, sir. I do apologize."

"No problem, Kathy."

"Heads up," the waitress whispered. "Front door. The Mouse has roared." She sauntered away.

Jared's head snapped around. "Well, I'll be damned."

"Jared?" Tabor asked.

"Mickey 'the Mouse' Mason," Jared said, a rough edge to his voice, "in the flesh."

Nick looked toward the door. "I don't believe it," he said. "He really looks like Mickey Mouse. Check out those ears, the nose, the eyebrows. The guy is a mouse. And those men on either side of him, by the way, are really gorillas."

"He has Finn," Tabor whispered. "That horrible man has my brother."

"Easy, Tabor," Jared said. "Look, it's obvious Mason knows you're here. I figure his men spotted you right off, reported back to him, and here he is. Nick, take Tabor up to my suite."

"No," she said. "I'm not going. I couldn't stand

being up there not knowing what's happening. I'll be fine with you, I promise. It just threw me for a minute to actually see the man who has Finn. Please, Jared, let me stay."

He gazed at her for a long moment. "All right. I don't like it, but . . . that guy is scum, Tabor, I don't even like the idea of your being in the same room with him."

Nick looked up at the ceiling and smiled.

"Well, let's go greet our lowlife guests," Jared said tightly. "Mouse must really be sweating about that list to show up like this. Nick, stay on one side of Tabor, I'll be on the other. Try to look mean."

"Me?" Tabor asked.

"No, darlin'," Jared said, smiling. "Nick."

Nick tugged on the lapels of his jacket and squared his broad shoulders. "I'm into my gorilla mode, chief."

"I'm now remembering why I retired from this lunacy," Jared said, shaking his head. "This is absurd."

"I'm cool," Nick said. "I'm really getting into my role. Let us venture forth, snare us a mouse, and get us a Finn."

"In a minute." Jared scanned the room, making eye contact with Trig, Spider, and a dozen others, four of whom were women. They all acknowledged Jared with barely discernible nods. "Okay, slow and easy."

The three started forward at a leisurely pace, Tabor trying to ignore her trembling legs and wildly beating heart. Mickey Mason and the two huge men with him had not moved from where they'd stopped about four feet inside the door.

"Hold it," Jared said quietly. Tabor and Nick quit walking.

"He's twenty feet away, Jared," Nick said.

"*He* comes to *me*," Jared said in a cold voice. "It's killing him to have to step onto my turf at all. He's going to have to go the whole distance."

"What if he refuses?" Tabor asked. "What if he gets angry and leaves?"

"He won't."

Several long minutes passed with neither group making a move. Tabor marveled at the fact that no one in the casino seemed to be paying any attention to the standoff.

"Is this dumb?" Nick asked out of the corner of his mouth. "I sure feel dumb."

"It's ridiculous," Jared said, "but necessary. Unbutton your jacket, Nick. You're supposed to be a pro."

"Oh. Sorry." Nick quickly undid the buttons. "There are just so many details to remember to be a good hood."

Jared was unable to keep from smiling. "That did it. The Mouse thinks I'm laughing at him. He's puffing up like a rooster and getting red in the face. The man is ticked. Stay loose. Here they come."

Oh, dear heaven, Tabor thought. If she fainted she'd never forgive herself. For as long as she could remember, Cat had told stories about men like those now approaching. But tales at her father's knee and actually being face-to-face with these people were two entirely different things. She had to stay calm, appear in total control for Finn's sake.

The three men stopped in front of Tabor, Jared, and Nick.

"Hello, Mickey," Jared said blandly. "Welcome to Miracles."

"You have something that belongs to me, Loring," Mason said. "I want it."

"Well, Mick, *you* have something that belongs to *me*."

"I thought you retired."

"This is a special occasion."

Mason's glance slid over Tabor. "Yes, I can see you've had pleasurable incentive to do one more job."

Jared's jaw tightened. "I'm a busy man, Mason. I don't have time to chat. State your business or get out."

"We'll talk privately."

"We'll talk right here. I retired because I was bored dealing with people like you. You're boring me, Mickey."

Oh, Jared, Tabor thought. Mickey Mason was getting furious, and Jared was really pushing.

"Damn you," Mason said harshly. "You're as arrogant as you always were. I want the list, Loring."

"And I get?" Jared asked.

"Finn O'Casey."

Yes! Tabor thought. Oh, please, Jared, say yes.

"Maybe," Jared said. "That list is worth a lot of money on the street."

"You take it on the street, you'll find O'Casey's body waiting for you."

"No," Tabor whispered.

"I'll tell you what, Mick," Jared said. "You can have the list because I really don't care to deal on the streets anymore. I'll take Finn O'Casey and be done with it. The list is bigger news than O'Casey, so the trade is mine to set up. I'll call you. Give me a number."

"You're losing it, Loring," Mason sneered. "I'm not giving you a number you can get an address for. *I'll* call *you*."

Jared shrugged. "Whatever." He reached inside his jacket for a pen and card and wrote on the back of the card. "My private number."

Mason took the card. "When?"

"Call me at noon tomorrow. I sleep late. Oh, and, Mick? I'm bored, remember? If Finn O'Casey isn't close by, I suggest you move him in. I'm really tired of this little game."

"I'm leaving now, Loring. Don't do anything stupid like trying to follow me."

"I wouldn't dream of it. You stay smart and keep Finn O'Casey healthy. Noon. Tomorrow. Don't make me wait, or I'll really get bored. Good night, Mason. You're cluttering up my casino."

Mason jerked his head at the two men with him, then after one more dark glare at Jared spun around and stalked out, the huge men lumbering after him.

"Got him," Jared said. "*He's* calling *me*."

"But why did you postpone the call until noon tomorrow?" Tabor asked. "Why do we have to wait so long?"

"I need the time to set up the equipment I need. A phone trace is good, but we've got a better, faster system. Mason will know exactly how long a trace takes, and won't talk beyond that. He thinks he has the edge. He doesn't. Nick, take Tabor up to my suite. I've got to round up the people I need. Tabor, go to bed, get some sleep."

"But . . ." she began.

He brushed his thumb across her cheek and smiled. "Go on. It's almost over. Hold on to that thought. It's almost all over." He walked away.

"All over," she said softly, watching as he disappeared into the crowd. "All of it."

"I don't think so," Nick mumbled.

"Pardon me?"

"Nothing. Come on, Tabor, I'll see you safely upstairs. Want to hear an Italian bedtime story? Hey, can you believe how much that guy really looked like Mickey Mouse?"

Tabor managed a small smile as she walked across the casino with Nick. Almost over, her mind echoed. Finn would be with her very soon. Almost *all* over. Oh, Jared.

Six

For Tabor the night was long, her sleep plagued by frightening nightmares that made no sense. Faceless men chased her through tangled jungles as she searched frantically for her father, for Finn, for Jared, as other people she didn't know called to her for help. The faster she ran, the less ground she covered, and suddenly everyone was screaming at her, telling her she must first find herself before she could reach those she sought.

Tabor woke with a start, sitting bolt upright in the bed, her heart pounding. She was tangled in the sheets, and tears were drying on her cheeks. She drew in a shuddering breath and looked quickly at the expanse of bed next to her.

Jared had not slept in the bed.

The clock read eight-thirty, and she hurried into the bathroom for a reviving shower that she hoped would wash away the horrors of her dreams.

By ten she had dressed in a khaki skirt and a safari jacket belted at the waist, braided her hair into a single plait, and eaten a light breakfast.

Where was Jared?

She paced restlessly around the large living room. The call from Mickey Mason was to come at noon. If Jared thought she was going to be kept locked up alone in that room while he negotiated for Finn's release, he had another think coming. Not a chance, buster.

She marched to the door, undid the lock, and yanked the door open. A tall burly man turned quickly to look at her.

"Good morning," she said. "Are you Pico or Joe?"

"I'm Joe. Was your breakfast all right, ma'am?"

"Yes, Joe, it was fine. I'd like you to take me to Mr. Loring now."

"I'm sorry, ma'am, but I can't do that. My orders are to stay right here."

"Then you stay here. Simply tell me where Mr. Loring is and I'll go myself."

"No, ma'am, I can't let you do that. You're to remain in the suite."

"Listen to me. I'm not a prisoner here, for heaven's sake. I want—I demand to see Jared."

"Tabor!"

She turned to see Jared striding down the hall toward her. The jacket to his tuxedo was flung over his arm, his shirt was half unbuttoned, he needed a shave, and his hair was tousled, as though he'd repeatedly raked his fingers through it.

"Glad to see you, Mr. Loring," Joe said, relief evident in his voice.

Jared stopped, looked at Tabor, at Joe, then back to Tabor. "What's going on here?"

He was tired, Tabor thought. His blue eyes were cloudy with fatigue and the small lines next to them were more pronounced than usual.

"I asked to be taken to where you were," she said.

"Joe has orders not to do that."

She frowned. "So I discovered. I informed him that I'm not a prisoner here, but it made no impression. Jared, I will not be left out of—"

"Let's go inside," he interrupted, taking her arm. "Thank you, Joe."

"Sure glad you showed up," Joe mumbled.

Jared closed the door, tossed his jacket onto a chair, and pulled his shirt free of his pants. Tabor folded her arms across her chest.

"I'll shower and change," he said.

"Wait," she said, raising one hand. "Let's get this straight right now. I won't be left here alone while you're talking to Mickey Mason."

He removed his shirt and dropped it on top of his jacket.

Do not look at that bare chest, Tabor told herself. She had to stand her ground, make it very clear to Jared that she wouldn't be excluded from what was taking place at noon.

"Tabor, I'll report right back to you the minute I've finished speaking with Mason." There was an impatient edge to Jared's voice.

"No. I have the right to be there."

Jared sighed and undid his belt.

"Quit taking your clothes off!" she yelled. "Oh, go ahead. I don't care if you strip down to your bare bottom, you're not going to distract me. I'm going with you to hear that call, Jared Loring."

His hands on his hips, he stared at her. She met his gaze steadily, praying he couldn't hear the wild beating of her heart. He nodded.

"Okay. But remember this, Tabor. What you see

in that room, you forget the minute we leave it. That includes equipment, people, everything."

"For Pete's sake, I'm Cat O'Casey's daughter. I'm not some bimbo who's going to run out to tell all to anyone who will listen. I grew up understanding the need for secrecy. I know who you are and you men of the night don't frighten me, nor does the world you move in."

Jared continued gazing at her for a long moment, various unreadable expressions flitting across his face.

"I'll shower and change," he said at last, "then I'll take you with me."

"Thank you," she said quietly. She paused. "You're very tired."

"We had a lot to do to get ready for this." He started across the room. "I won't be long."

So intense, Tabor mused, watching him go. Jared was giving maximum effort to Finn's safe return, and he'd never even met Finn. So very, very intense, and that would be how he would love—if he'd ever allow himself to. He cared for her, she knew he did, but what would it take to get him to look deeper within himself, discover his true feelings for her? Did he love her? Was that love hiding in the shadows of his soul, behind the walls, or was she hoping for something that wasn't even there? It could very well be that she'd never know.

She sank into the sofa and pressed her fingers to her throbbing temples. It was almost over, her mind echoed, all of it.

Jared stood in the shower and let the hot water beat against his body. He could feel some of the tension ebb from his muscles, his energy returning after the long and tedious night. Tabor's words filtered into his mind and repeated themselves over and over.

I know who you are.

And she did know who he was, he realized. He'd grown accustomed to skillfully sidestepping questions from women he associated with, knew how to keep so much of himself hidden from them. He turned conversations around, directing the focus onto them, and they basked in his attention, never seeming to notice how little they learned about him.

I know who you are.

And then there was Tabor, he mused, closing his eyes as the water poured over him. His life had changed from the moment he'd seen her. Her plea for help had taken him back down a road he'd thought he'd left behind him forever. Yet, it hadn't been a disturbing journey, because Tabor had been there, not judging him, but respecting who he'd been and who he now was. They'd come together in their lovemaking with no secrets between them, no facades or unanswered questions. And it had been the most beautiful lovemaking he'd ever experienced.

Jared stepped from the shower, and by the time he'd dried his hair and shaved, felt a hundred percent better than when he'd come dragging down that hall. There was still a great deal to do before this was finished, but they were ahead of the game, ahead of Mickey Mason.

I know who you are.

He frowned as he dressed in jeans and a light blue cotton dress shirt. Tabor's words were obviously not going to leave him alone. Why they were haunting him, he wasn't quite sure. Yes, she was special, different from any woman he'd ever known, but he felt he was missing some message, not seeing the piece that would complete a very complicated puzzle.

Well, he decided, it was all going on hold for now. The hours ahead had to be directed to the mission at hand—the safe return of Finn O'Casey.

He entered the living room and smiled at Tabor. "I'm a new man."

"You look better, more refreshed," she said, matching his smile. He looked wonderful. She wanted him to hold her and kiss her, to erase the last lingering ghosts of her frightening nightmares. "Have you eaten?"

"Yes. We'll go in a few minutes. I called a break to give everyone a chance to get a second wind."

"I'm sorry I pitched such a fit, Jared, but I just couldn't be left here alone."

"I understand. I wasn't thinking it through. I forget sometimes that you know as much as you do about the inner workings of these things."

"Does it bother you that I know? You seemed rather uncomfortable when I first told you."

"Not uncomfortable, just surprised. And, no, it doesn't bother me. It's . . . nice." He shook his head. "Lord, what an inane word. *Nice*. That doesn't even come close. It's difficult to explain, Tabor. I've never been able to totally relax around . . . well, around women, because I was on guard against questions, had to weigh and measure what I said. It's not like that with you."

But some of the walls were still there, she thought. The walls around his heart were high and solid. She didn't know how to get through them, or over them.

And unless she did, he'd never know of the sunshine she could bring to his life.

"Tabor? What's wrong? You look sad all of a sudden." He drew her into his arms. "Would a kiss make it better?"

"I think that's exactly what I need."

Jared's kiss worked its magic, lifting the last of the gloom of the night up and away from Tabor, leaving her free to savor the ecstasy of being in his arms, feeling his hard body pressed to hers. She answered the demands of his mouth, and made demands of her own as desire bubbled within her.

When he lifted his head, Jared chuckled. "Lady, you are a dangerous weapon. You could make me forget all about what I'm supposed to be doing."

"You're doing what you're supposed to be doing, kissing me."

"We'll pick up where we left off . . . later. We'd better get to my office. Everyone should be back by now." He brushed his thumbs over her cheeks. "You really do know who I am."

"Yes. Yes, Jared, I believe I do."

He looked at her intently. Tabor tried to read his expression, decipher what was in his eyes, but failed.

"Let's go." He stepped away from her and started toward the door.

She watched him for a moment, then followed.

The office was busy, with people moving around and speaking in low voices. Tabor recognized some of the faces, others she didn't. Jared made no introductions other than to say, "This is Tabor, Finn's sister, Cat's daughter." She received smiles and nods of greeting, then everyone got back to work.

At the end of the room three men sat in front of three computers that had a jumble of wires and cables leading from them to a large screen. Another maze of cables led to a box on the floor, then on to the telephone on Jared's desk.

Nick, dressed in jeans and a brown polo shirt, walked over to her and Jared.

"Hello, Nick," she said, smiling at him.

"Isn't this something?" he said. "It's like a top-secret war room."

"That's exactly what it is," Jared said dryly.

"True. That equipment is so sophisticated it blows my mind. I just about have it figured out though."

"Nick has a photographic memory, Tabor," Jared said. "He may overload his brain circuits with this stuff though."

"No joke," Nick said. "Do you know, Tabor, that just because I can remember every card I've seen dealt, I've been banned from the blackjack tables. Now, I ask you, is that fair?"

Jared laughed. "Damn right it's fair, unless you want Tucker and me to go bankrupt because of your winnings."

"Tucker," Nick said. "He doesn't know anything about what's going on here. Are you going to tell him, Jared?"

"When it's all over. He's got enough on his mind waiting for Alison to have that baby."

"Yes, he does, and he's certainly too preoccupied to be worrying about the bet you two made."

"I've been so busy, I forgot about that," Jared said. "There's still over a week to go."

"Is there?" Nick asked, sliding a quick smile at Tabor, who was totally confused.

"Well, yeah," Jared said, "I have that date tattooed on my brain. I—"

"Ready to test, Jared," a man called.

"Let's do it," Jared said. "We're cutting it close here. Nick, you're up."

Nick crossed the room and picked up the receiver to a telephone. He punched in some numbers, said "Call in," then hung up. A hush fell over the room.

"Watch that screen," Jared said quietly to Tabor. "Mouse knows exactly how soon to get off the line so he can't be traced. This is where we get him."

"But if you can't trace his call . . ." she started.

"Just watch the screen." The telephone on Jared's desk rang, and he walked over to it and picked it up.

"Loring," he said.

The first computer began to hum, then a series of numbers flashed on the screen. In the next instant a map of the United States came into view.

"How's life, Frannie?" Jared asked. "Enjoying your retirement and those grandkids? . . . You've got six now? Good for you."

The state of Florida began to blink with a bright light. The second computer hummed, Florida filled the screen, then another light blinked.

"Me?" Jared was saying. "I'm fine, just fine. You should come out here and win some money in my casino, Frannie."

The third computer came alive, and pictures rushed across the screen. Tabor gasped as an address was printed out.

"Frannie," Jared said, watching the screen, "you're at two one seven Winding Creek Road. . . . I love you, babe, you're my best girl. . . . What? . . ."

"Trace kicked in on the phone," someone said.

"You bet, Frannie," Jared said. "If I ever do one of these again, I'll include you. That's a promise. 'Bye." He hung up. "We're gonna get him, by damn. We're gonna get Mickey by his mouse ears."

A whoop of delight sounded from the people in the room. Tabor walked over to Jared and was joined by Nick.

"That was incredible," she said. "I've never seen anything so effective. Cat didn't tell me about this equipment."

"I doubt he was ever in a position to need it, or even to see it work."

"How did you get it here so quickly?"

"Oh, that." Jared shrugged. "I developed this system myself, wrote the programs for the computers. I just sort of kept copies for myself, along with the cables and other equipment, when I retired. I turned the program over to the feds too. One for them, one for me."

"You are a genius," she said, her eyes sparkling.

He dropped a fast kiss onto her lips, then smiled at her. "Think so?"

"Naw," Nick said, "how tough could it have been to write that program?" He rolled his eyes. "Who am I kidding? It boggles my mind."

"The bottom line is," Jared said, his smile gone, "it's our ace in the hole for getting Finn. Mason may look like a spaced-out mouse, but he's sharp, tough, and ruthless. Even though he's desperate to get that list back, he'd pull a double-cross without blinking. He doesn't like loose ends, and that includes people who know what he's been doing. When we move, we move fast. Tabor, you'll be here in my suite with Nick. Both Pico and Joe will be on the door, and there will be guards at the elevator and stairs. Stay put."

"I want to go with you," she said.

"Don't even think about it. All my concentration has to be on getting Finn out. I have to know that you're safe, Tabor. I have to."

Nick smiled. "Ah, that's so sweet. Isn't that sweet, Tabor?" Both Tabor and Jared glared at him. He shrugged. "I thought it was sweet. Italians are very romantic, you know."

"Okay, let's reset the equipment," Jared said loudly enough for everyone to hear him. "Remember, when Mason calls, don't even breathe heavy. I want him to think I'm alone. We've got less than fifteen minutes. Be ready."

It seemed to Tabor that time turned into a sadistic enemy. Fifteen minutes was an eternity, and her heart beat painfully with every slow-moving tick of the clock. The room was quiet, no one spoke or shifted positions, or even cleared his throat. Tabor sat in a chair next to Jared's desk, and Nick stood behind her like a statue. The tension in the room built to a crushing weight.

At twelve o'clock the telephone rang.

Tabor gasped and jumped in her chair.

"Here we go," Jared said, and reached for the receiver. "Loring."

The first computer began to hum quietly.

"Mason. Make it quick, Loring. I'm not falling for a trace. You know it, and I know it."

"Phone traces are kid stuff, Mickey," Jared said.

The state of Nevada glowed brightly on the screen. The second computer hummed into action.

"Where and when, Loring?" Mickey asked. "Hurry up."

"Tonight. Eight o'clock. The parking lot at Hoover Dam."

Nevada was magnified on the screen. A light blinked steadily.

"Bring the girl," Mason said.

Jared stiffened. "What the hell for?"

The third computer kicked in.

"Insurance. You won't want any slipup, any gunfire, with your new lady in the way. Bring her."

"Yeah, fine," Jared said.

Pictures blurred the screen, then an address began to chug its way across the green expanse.

"Don't pull anything cute, Loring."

"I wouldn't dream of it, Mason. This stuff bores me now, remember?"

"That's enough talk. A trace will start in ten seconds. Eight o'clock. Tonight. Bring her." Mason hung up.

"Trace got a dial tone," someone said.

Jared slammed the phone down and stood up. Trig was spreading a map out on a table.

"Jared?" Tabor asked, starting to rise.

"Easy," Nick said. He placed his hands on her shoulders and gently eased her back into her chair.

"There," Trig said, his finger on the map. "That's the address that's on the screen. Those are cabins, boss. You know, vacation places in an isolated spot. It's—let's see—about fifteen miles out of town."

"Let's hit the road," Jared said. "You have the weapons?"

"Everything we need. It's you, me, and Marcus."

"Keep your fingers crossed, people," Jared said. "We're on our way. You did great, all of you." He crossed the room to Tabor. "Go to the suite with Nick."

"Yes," she said, nodding. "Be careful. Please, Jared? Please, be careful."

He smiled at her. "Always am. Wait for me, Tabor." He brushed his lips over hers. "I'll be back before you know it, and I'll have your brother with me."

"I'll be waiting," she whispered.

He looked at her for a long moment.

"Boss?"

Jared snapped his head around. "What? Yeah, let's go."

He left the room with Trig and Marcus, a tall, dark-haired man, and the others began to talk among themselves, smiling and nodding as they glanced at the screen.

"Ready to go to the suite?" Nick asked Tabor.

She started to rise, then realized her legs were trembling and she took a steadying breath. *Wait for me, Tabor,* Jared had said. What strange words for him to have spoken, she thought. Of course she would wait for him. Not just until he brought Finn back, but forever. She'd wait for Jared Loring forever. She loved him.

"Are you all right, Tabor?" Nick asked.

"Yes. Yes, I'm fine," she said, finally standing. She managed a weak smile. "It just all caught up with me for a moment, I guess."

Nick put his arm gently around her shoulders. "You've been terrific. A lot of people wouldn't have held up this well, me included. Before you know it, you and Finn will be having a great reunion. We'll break out the finest champagne in the place."

"You're very sweet," she said as they left the office.

He laughed. "I know. Kind of gets you in the old ticker, doesn't it?"

She laughed as well, and realized Nick had managed to snap her out of her semifrozen state of fear. Nick Capoletti was a dear, wonderful man, so open and refreshing. He seemed to embrace life as it came. Oh, why couldn't she have fallen in love with a man like Nick? But, oh, no, not Tabor O'Casey. She'd lost her heart to a deep, complicated, intense person named Jared Loring.

"Just down this hall and around the corner," Nick said pleasantly, "and you'll be home, safe and sound."

"Home?" she repeated, looking up at him.

"Yes," he said, suddenly serious, "home."

"You know, don't you? You know that I . . ." Her voice trailed off.

"That you're in love with Jared? Yes."

"Oh, Nick, please don't say anything to him. This is difficult enough without him knowing."

"Hey, it's not my place to tell him. That's your job. I'm not going to open my mouth and inform him that *he's* in love with *you* either."

She stopped dead in her tracks. "What?"

"Come on, keep walking. My orders are to get you safely inside that suite with the big boys standing guard outside."

Tabor started walking again. "Nick, you're wrong. Jared isn't in love with me. He's made it clear that he prefers to live his life alone, and he makes no commitments or promises."

Nick shrugged. "So, he's a little dense. Even sharp guys like Jared aren't perfect, you know. Well, *I'm* perfect, but Jared has a flaw or two. Just give him some time to come out of the ether. He's dense but not stupid. He'll figure out that he's in love with you."

"You're crazy," Tabor said, shaking her head.

"I am not," Nick said indignantly. "I'm adorable. Ask Turtle. She tells me three times a day that I'm adorable. Anyway, Jared is in love with you, you're in love with him, and that is that. I think it's terrific. We Italians are very romantic, you know. There's nothing we like better than a romantic love story. Well, pasta is high on our list too. We're nuts about pasta. I had a cousin who . . ."

Tabor only half heard Nick's story about a cousin who detested pasta, and the Capoletti wrath the cousin had endured. Her mind was buzzing with Nick's statement that Jared loved her. She embraced the thought in one moment, rejected it as nonsense the next.

She knew Jared cared about her, but could he be in love with her? No, he . . . was it possible? No, he . . . oh, could it be true? No, he . . . but Jared had said *Wait for me, Tabor*. What had he meant, really meant, by that?

She moaned. "Oh, my mind is turning into scrambled eggs."

"Scrambled eggs?" Nick said thoughtfully. "You know, I'm hungry. First order of business when we get to the suite will be to have something to eat. Let's quicken our step, my dear. Nourishment beckons."

And so did home, Tabor thought. Home was where the heart was, and it was just around the corner in Jared's suite.

Marcus drove the Blazer with expertise, and Jared gazed out the side window at the city whizzing by.

Why had he said what he had to Tabor, he asked himself. To tell her to wait for him hadn't made sense. Where in the hell did he think she'd disappear to while he was gone? He was bringing her brother back to her, for God's sake.

No, he reluctantly admitted, the words he'd spoken to Tabor had come from a different place in his mind. They'd had nothing to do with Finn. He'd had a compelling need to say those words, and for the life of him he couldn't figure out why.

The city gave way to desert, and a few minutes later Marcus turned off the main road onto a bumpy one that led to the foothills of the mountains in the distance.

He was not, Jared vowed, going to think about Tabor for one more second until Finn was safely out of Mickey Mason's hands. Jared knew from long years of experience that his total concentration had to be on what he was doing. He also knew, and didn't like one damn bit, that this was the first time in his life he'd ever had to forcibly pull his mind away from thoughts of a woman. This wasn't like him at all. What was Tabor O'Casey doing to him?

Trig leaned forward in the backseat, a map in his hands. "We're getting close, boss. The place we're looking for is a mile or so up ahead. How considerate of the Mouse to pick a spot with plenty of trees for cover. He's a gem, isn't he?"

"A real sweetheart," Jared said. "Okay, Marcus, pull over anywhere along here that you can hide the vehicle."

"Yep," Marcus said.

A few minutes later the three were standing by the Blazer, which was covered by the low-hanging branches of several trees. The three men had guns in holsters clipped to the backs of their belts, and Trig passed out rifles.

"Stay together, stay low," Jared said. "We'll fan out once we can see what's happening at the cabin."

"Damn, it's hot," Trig said. "Forget what I said about the Mouse being considerate. Why couldn't he have snatched Finn O'Casey in the winter?"

"We'll speak to Mason about that," Jared said. "Ready?"

"I guess," Trig said. "I'm melting into a grease spot."

"Marcus?"

"Yep," Marcus said.

"You shouldn't have brought Marcus, boss," Trig said. "He talks too much."

"Let's go."

They moved swiftly and quietly, experience not forgotten as they crept through the trees, breaking no twigs under their feet, causing minimal noise as they brushed back branches. The heat was oppressive. Sweat glued their shirts to their chests and backs, and glistened on their faces.

"There," Trig finally whispered. "That's the cabin. One car. They're in there."

"You two stay put," Jared said. "I'll work my way around to get a look in that side window."

"Yep," Marcus said.

"Okay, boss," Trig said. "Watch yourself. We'll cover you from here."

Jared nodded and started out, crouching low as he moved through the trees. Adrenaline pumped through his veins in a familiar surge. His muscles were tense, his senses alert for any sign of danger.

Sights, sounds, smells, were magnified. All was quiet except for the normal noises of nature: birds chirping, small animals scurrying through the underbrush.

He arrived at the edge of the trees and saw he had only a clearing of a dozen feet to cross to get to the dusty window of the cabin. Bent over, he ran quickly to the side of the small building and hunkered beneath the window, wiping away the sweat dripping into his eyes. He inched upward and squinted to see through the layer of dust on the windowpane. He frowned deeply as he studied the scene inside the cabin.

As quickly and quietly as he'd come, Jared retraced his steps, returning to where Trig and Marcus waited for him.

"Well?" Trig asked. "What's the scoop?"

"Weird," Jared said. "There's a big dark-haired guy sprawled in a chair. He looks like he's out cold, or dead. There's another one slouched over a table."

"And O'Casey?"

"Spread-eagled on his back on the floor, not moving. He's tall, well-built, blond, looks like Tabor even through a dusty window. It's Finn, all right."

"Do you think they're all dead, boss?" Trig asked. "Hell, that doesn't make sense. The other guys have to be the Mouse's men. Why would he waste his own people? And where the hell is the Mouse?"

"He's not in there. It's a one-room cabin, plus a bathroom. The bathroom door was open, and there's no one in there."

"Do you think it's a trap? Hell no, it's not a trap. They couldn't have known we were coming."

"It doesn't feel right," Jared said. "My little voice isn't whispering, it's screaming at me." He wiped the sweat from his face. "Well, let's get inside. Marcus, take the back door. Trig, you and I will go in the front. Marcus, get in position. Wait for me to whistle once, then go in."

"Yep," Marcus said.

"Definitely doesn't feel right," Jared muttered. "Damn."

"So, where in the hell is the Mouse?" Trig asked. "I don't like it, boss, don't like it at all."

"Well, there's only one way to find out," Jared said. "Let's move."

Crouched low, rifles in their hands, the three made their way to the edge of the trees by the cabin. Marcus continued on while Jared and Trig waited for him to get to the rear of the building. When he was in position, Jared nodded and he and Trig crept across the clearing, keeping their bodies as close to the ground as possible. Jared eased onto the wooden porch, testing it for creaking boards. Again they crouched to pass under a window, then flattened themselves against the weathered wood of the cabin on either side of the door. Jared jerked one thumb at his own chest, and Trig nodded in understanding.

Jared whistled low, then whirled and kicked the door open. In a blur of motion he rolled into the room, coming to rest belly down, his elbows planted on the floor, rifle at the ready. Trig was seconds behind him, and Marcus was in the same position a heartbeat later.

No one moved.

Silence hung in the air like an ominous dark cloud.

Jared stood cautiously, his rifle trained on the man sprawled in the chair. Trig and Marcus stood as well.

"Trig," Jared said, "check Finn. Marcus, look at that guy at the table." Jared moved to the man in the chair.

"Finn is out cold," Trig said.

"So is this joker," Jared said. "Marcus?"

"Yep."

Jared crossed the room to the table and picked up one of three mugs. He smelled the remaining coffee in the mug, then dipped a finger into the liquid and tasted it.

"They've been drugged." His eyes narrowed and his voice was low and cold when he spoke again. "Damn that Mason. God, I can't believe this. He set us up. He figured I'd have something more going for me than a simple phone trace. He's turning over two of his own bozos to get what he wants."

"You've lost me, boss," Trig said. "We've got Finn O'Casey, and the Mouse doesn't have the list."

"Mason had no intention of keeping the deal we made to switch at Hoover Dam," Jared said tightly. "He doesn't underestimate anyone . . . ever. He just redealt the cards, and he's holding all the aces."

"We've got Finn, boss," Trig said, still obviously confused.

"Dammit, Trig, don't you see?" Jared roared. *"Mason has Tabor!"*

Seven

Jared felt as though everything was moving in slow motion, gobbling up great chunks of precious time. While Marcus went to get the Blazer, Jared and Trig tied up the two burly, unconscious men. Trig discovered the telephone that Mason had called from torn out of the wall, and also saw a back road leading from the cabin. That explained why they had seen no sign of a car leaving the area as they'd approached.

Jared propped Finn O'Casey up against the wall in a sitting position, then pressed cold, wet cloths to his face and neck. When Marcus arrived with the Blazer, he and Trig lugged Mason's two men outside while Jared continued to revive a now groaning Finn.

Through it all one word screamed in Jared's mind. Tabor!

Dear God, he thought as he continued working on Finn. Mickey Mason had Tabor. Oh, how clever Jared had decided he was with his fancy equipment and confident statements that he was one step ahead of the Mouse. But Mason had been faster and better, anticipating Jared's every move. Like a cocky rookie agent, Jared had strutted his stuff, never dreaming for a second that Mason had outsmarted him.

And now Tabor was paying the price.

Hot fury and cold fear churned within Jared like a twisting knife, filling him with pain. Tabor. Oh, God, Tabor!

He had to calm down, he told himself. He had to think clearly, plan his next move. There was no room, no time, for emotions rushing out of control. Tabor needed him to act precisely in order to free her.

"Finn," Jared said, slapping him lightly on the face. "Finn, come on, wake up."

"Yeah, I'm coming," Finn mumbled. "Five more minutes, Tabor. We won't . . . we won't be late for school if . . . I sleep . . . five more minutes."

Tabor's name coming from Finn's lips slammed against Jared's mind. He stared at Finn, studying the younger man's handsome features through the grime and several days growth of beard, seeing the O'Casey family resemblance. Finn was tall, over six feet, and had a nicely muscled physique without being a bulging mass from pumping iron. His hair, now dirty, was obviously thick and blond like Tabor's.

This was Tabor's brother, Jared thought. He'd known her since she was born, had looked after her, been her protector, her hero. This was Finn, whose brave actions had brought Tabor to Jared for help. How in the hell was he going to tell Finn that Tabor was now the one in danger because Jared Loring had underestimated a sleazeball?

God, Tabor, Jared thought, *I'm so damn sorry!*

"Finn," he said. "Open your eyes. We've got to get out of here. We have to go to Tabor, Finn."

"What?" Finn's lashes fluttered on his tanned, sweaty cheeks. "Tabor?"

"Finn, I'm Jared Loring. Jared, remember? Tabor came to me for help to get you out of this. Come on. Wake up."

Finn slowly opened his eyes. They were brown like Tabor's, now cloudy with the effects of the drug.

"Tabor," Finn said, his voice slurred. "Jared Loring."

Jared slung one of Finn's arms around his own shoulders, then circled Finn's waist with his other arm.

"On your feet. Ready?"

"Tired."

"I know, but we've got to get moving."

"Where's Tabor?"

The knife twisted tighter in Jared's gut. "Get up, Finn."

"Yeah, I'm up. Aren't I? No, I'm not."

"The meat is in the Blazer, boss," Trig said, coming into the cabin. "How's Finn?"

"Stoned. Help me get him on his feet. We've got to get back to town, get Tabor . . . come on, give me a hand."

"We'll get her, boss," Trig said, slinging Finn's other arm around him. "We lost this round, but we're not down for the count. We'll get her."

Jared met Trig's gaze, and Trig nodded decisively.

"Hey, Finn," Trig said, switching his attention to the other man, "you sure look like your sister. No, forget that. She's pretty. You're a sweaty mess. On your feet, kid, we've got places to go, people to see."

"Now," Jared said to Trig. "Up."

Finn was hauled to his feet, where he teetered unsteadily and groaned.

"The hell with this," Jared said. "We're wasting too much time." He leveled his shoulder into Finn's stomach and hoisted him up, Finn's arms dangling down Jared's back.

A few minutes later Finn was propped up in the backseat with Trig sitting next to him. The two tied-up men were lying in the flat area behind the seat. Jared got into the front seat and Marcus slid behind the wheel.

"Weapons?" Jared asked.

"Got 'em," Trig said.

"Let's get the hell out of here."

"Yep," Marcus said.

They sped away from the cabin and Finn slid down in the seat, his head resting on the top, his eyes closed.

"Let him sleep it off," Jared said.

"Doesn't look like they roughed him up," Trig said. "He's in good shape, though, might have handled whatever they dished out while he was stalling for time, waiting to be sure Tabor got to you."

"Hell of a lot of good it did her," Jared said, shaking his head. "Damn that Mason. When I get my hands on him, I'm going to—"

"Easy, boss. The Mouse wants you mad as hell, so you'll screw up. He was shootin' in the dark, you know, counting on you being able to track him when he called. It was an outside chance, and he pegged it right. You've got to reshuffle the deck, deal the aces back to our side. We'll give you the Mouse when this is over. Right now . . . think. What in the hell are we gonna do? We gotta have a plan."

"Yep," Marcus said.

Jared rubbed his hands across his face. "Yeah, you're right, I'm losing it here, but the thought of Tabor . . ." He took a deep breath and let it out slowly. "Okay. How's Finn?"

"Sleeping like a baby," Trig said, patting Finn on the head. "You can bet those two sides of beef in the back were hired off the street for this job. The Mouse isn't about to turn over any doughheads who know anything about his operation."

"Marcus," Jared said, "do you know where Jazzy Jones's place is?"

"Yep."

"Go to the alley behind Jazzy's, and we'll give him those two. He'll know who to call to come get them."

'Yep."

"Boss," Trig said, "do you think the Mouse is holding Tabor at Miracles?"

"That's the first order of business, Trig. We have to find out. Damn, Nick was with her. What in the hell did Mason do to Nick? And Pico and Joe, and the guys on the elevator and stairs? Nobody was expecting Mason to show up there, and I'd say he caught everyone off guard. As much as I hate it, we're going to have to move slow and easy until we get a handle on what's going on."

Trig laced his hands over his chest, leaned back in the seat, and smiled. "My man is thinking. I knew you'd get it together, boss."

"Yeah, right," Jared said dryly. "I've done a terrific job so far."

"Don't be so hard on yourself. This is just a minor setback. You've been in tight spots before and come out the winner."

He'd been in tight spots, Jared thought, staring out the side window. He'd taken chances, big chances, knowing that the only one who would pay a price if it went bad would be him. But this time there was Tabor to think of. Every move he made, every decision, had to be focused on her safety. Nothing was going to happen to his Tabor! If Mason had touched her, put his filthy hands on her . . . easy, Loring. He had to stay calm, in control. What he did in the next few hours would be the most important actions in his entire life. What he did he'd be doing for Tabor.

"Tabor," Finn mumbled, then lifted his head. "Ohhh, Lord. My head is falling off."

Jared shifted in the seat to look back at Finn. "Finn, I'm Jared Loring."

Finn pressed the heels of his hands to his temples. "Thank God for that. I was counting on you to pull this off, Jared."

"I didn't . . . yet. But I'm going to. What kind of shape are you in? Besides having a headache. Did they work you over?"

"Some. My ribs are sore, bruised but not broken. I kept pretending that I passed out. I was buying time so Tabor could get to you. Did you find the list?"

"Yes, we've got it, but Mason has Tabor."

"What?" Finn said, sitting up straight.

"That's the only way to figure it," Jared said. "Mason called me from the cabin, then headed out the back road."

Finn nodded, then winced at the pain in his head. "I heard the call. Then he pulled a gun and forced me and"—he looked over his shoulder—"those two guys to drink some coffee. I saw him go out the back door just before I faded out. I thought you were meeting him at eight tonight."

"So did I. Mason second-guessed me on this. He didn't know how I'd trace that call, just counted on my being able to do it. I thought I had him cold. While I was charging out to the cabin like the Marines, the Mouse was strolling into Miracles as if he owned the place. What we don't know is if he's still there, or took Tabor out."

"Damn," Finn said.

"No joke. Marcus, there's Jazzy's up ahead. Let's dump this excess baggage we're carrying."

"Yep."

If Jazzy Jones thought there was anything unusual about Jared showing up at his back door to deposit two groaning, partially conscious muscle men, he didn't give any indication of it. The wiry little man said he'd have the pair picked up, and Jared's name wouldn't be mentioned. Jared pressed money into Jazzy's hand, and business was completed.

The next stop was a telephone booth in a park that was deserted due to the extreme heat. Jared called Miracles and asked to speak to Mrs. Tuttle.

"Mrs. Tuttle."

"Jared."

"Hi, sweetie pie. Where are you? Do you have Finn O'Casey? That was one smooth sting you pulled on the Mouse."

"Wrong," Jared said. "It backfired. Put me on hold and ring my office."

"What do you mean, it backfired?"

"Not now, Turtle. See if anyone is in my office."

"They all went to get some sleep, but I'll check. Sit tight." A few moments later she came back on the line. "No one answers."

"All right. Now ring my suite. Say you have a long-distance call for me. Ask whoever answers if they know when I'll be back. Turtle, listen carefully to see if you recognize who's speaking, and also listen for anything in the background."

"Gotcha. Hold on."

Jared drummed his fingers impatiently on the ledge in the booth, acutely aware that the rhythm of his thudding heart was faster than that of his fingers.

"Jared?"

"Was anyone there? Who answered the phone?"

"Tabor."

Jared narrowed his eyes. "Arrogant bastard. He's sitting right in my living room. How did Tabor sound?"

"Quiet, you know, sort of dulled out. She said she didn't know when you'd be back, but since she'd be waiting for you, she'd have you call me to get the message. I didn't hear any background noise. Jared, what happened?"

"Mason is smarter than I gave him credit for, Turtle. I've got Finn, but Mason is in my suite holding Tabor, Nick, and probably Pico and Joe."

"Well, damn his hide!" Turtle yelled.

"I intend to do more than that," Jared said tightly. "He's delivered his message through Tabor. He's waiting for me to show up. Turtle, wake everyone who is Code Dark Blue. Have them go to the small office downstairs. Tell them to move casually, not give any impression that the troops are gathering. I'll be there in fifteen minutes."

"Okay. Jared, you'll get Tabor out of this."

"I have to, Turtle. God, I . . ."

"I know, honey," she said gently. "But you'll do it. And Tabor knows it too." She hung up.

Jared kept the receiver pressed to his ear for a moment, hearing the dial tone and seeing visions of Tabor in his mind.

Tabor knew he'd get her safely away from Mason? Yes, she probably believed he'd do exactly that. She trusted him. She'd trusted him with the most precious thing she possessed—herself. When they'd made love she'd given of herself completely, holding nothing back, allowing him to carry her away into ecstasy, knowing he'd bring her safely back. That was trust in its purest, most beautiful form.

And beyond that, he realized, she'd trusted him to rescue her brother, whom she dearly loved. Now she was waiting for him to come for her and, by damn, he was going to get her out of there!

He slammed the receiver into place and strode back to the Blazer, sliding onto the front seat and pulling the door closed in the same motion.

"Mason is in my suite at Miracles," he said. "Tabor answered the phone when I had Turtle ring the room. We can only assume that Nick, Pico, and Joe are in there too. No telling where the guards from the elevator and stairs are, or how many men Mason has with him. Marcus, drive to Miracles, but come in the back way. We'll go in through the kitchen so Mason can't see us from any of the windows in my suite."

"Yep," Marcus said, pressing on the gas pedal.

"Trig," Jared went on, "when we get there, go to the main terminal box and disconnect the power to the security system for my suite. Make sure you get it all, especially the camera over the door. Then come to the small office downstairs. The Code Dark Blue people will be there."

"Okay, boss."

"What do you want me to do, Jared?" Finn asked. "That's my sister that creep has."

Jared sighed. "I know, Finn. I've been hearing that from Tabor, that it was her brother who was in trouble, and she wanted to be in on everything that was happening. Can you use a gun?"

"Yes. Cat saw to that."

"How's your head? Your ribs?"

"Not bad."

"All right, you're in. Lord knows I owe you that much."

"Hey," Finn said, "no one is blaming you for this snafu, Jared. Hell, that was smooth work the way you knew where I was so fast after Mason's call."

"He has Tabor," Jared said roughly.

"Yeah, but—"

Trig touched Finn on the arm and shook his head, indicating that Finn shouldn't say any more. Finn frowned and kept silent. No one spoke the rest of the way to Miracles.

At the casino Trig disappeared to tend to the power box while Jared, Finn, and Marcus went down the side hall to the small office. They could hear the noise and buzz of voices from the casino floor, but to Jared all that was a world away, a place that had nothing to do with him. The office was filled with quiet, grim-faced people.

"This is Finn O'Casey," Jared said to the group. "We got him out, and the Mouse came in. I assume Turtle told you that Mason is in my suite holding Tabor." Everyone nodded. "Nick, Pico, and Joe may be in there too."

The door opened and Trig entered. "I pulled the plug on the security, boss. Your private elevator came down because I yanked the juice. The guards from there and the stairs were in it, tied up and gagged. I unwound 'em, and they said the Mouse has two muscles with him. One guard said he saw Pico and Joe being shoved into your suite."

"Okay, Trig. That's about how I figured it, except I didn't know how many men Mason had."

"Two is a very small number," Spider said. "I could go up on the roof, come over the side, and in a window of your suite."

"No, it's too risky. If Mason gets nervous, he might start shooting. We have our own people in there." Tabor was in there. "We'll have to play this very close to the cuff." He paused. "In fact, we'll have to play it straight up."

"Meaning?" Finn asked.

"Give Mason what he wants," Jared said, looking at Finn.

"Oh, now wait a minute. You're talking about the list. No way, Jared. My father wanted that list delivered to the proper people. Tabor isn't going to go for your trading the list for her."

"She isn't going to be too thrilled with me if I get

her killed either, O'Casey," Jared said, his voice rising. Killed. Tabor? Oh, God, no! "We do this my way."

"Damn," Finn said, raking a hand through his hair.

"I don't like it any more than you do. Trig, is my elevator out of commission?"

"Won't budge, boss."

"Good. Divide up and cover every entrance to this place. Look casual, not as though you're on guard duty. Now, listen. If Mason leaves with any of our people, let him go. Understand? No guns are to be drawn on the casino floor under any circumstances, not even if Mason's with his own guys. If he saunters out across the casino, let him go."

"Hell," someone said.

"We're not risking the lives of innocent people," Jared said. "Trig, Marcus, Finn, stay off the floor. You look lousy and you'll make people nervous. You three will come up the service stairs with me. Trig, get Finn a gun. Any questions?"

"We're giving the Mouse a free ticket out of here, Jared," someone said. "Fat chance of him using a back door. He'll strut across the casino and be gone. This stinks."

"It's not wonderful," Jared said, "but it's the only game in town. Unless . . ." He narrowed his eyes and paced in front of the desk for several minutes.

Everyone watched Jared like a group of people intently studying a tennis match. Back and forth. Back and forth. Finally Jared stopped.

"How many of you smoke?" he asked.

Trig laughed. "Time out, folks, while we take a

health survey. Nasty habit, that smokin'. Bad for your body, you know what I mean?" Jared glared at him. "Sorry, boss. Okay, you jokers, if you smoke, confess now, or be strung up by your thumbs."

"Give it a rest, Trigger," Spider said. "You talk enough for twenty-five chatterboxes."

"Yep," Marcus said.

"People," Jared said wearily, "how many of you smoke?"

Eight hands shot into the air.

"Fine. Give your lighters or matches to Trig, Finn, and Marcus." He waited as the instructions were carried out. "Now, remember, no guns on the floor. If any of our people are with Mason, regardless of what door he uses, let him go. Stay cool and loose no matter what happens. I picked you carefully for Code Dark Blue. Don't blow it. Lives are at stake here." Tabor. Nick. Tabor. Pico and Joe. Tabor. Tabor. *Tabor!* "Let's go. Trig, Finn, Marcus, we're first. The rest of you leave two at a time."

Trig got a holstered gun out of the desk drawer and handed it to Finn, then the four left the office. They walked down the side corridor to the service stairs and began the trek upward, Jared in the lead. No one spoke.

Whatever it took, Jared vowed fiercely, he would get Tabor safely away from Mickey Mason. Nothing was going to happen to Tabor O'Casey. *Nothing!*

At the top of the stairs he stopped, unclipped his holster from his belt, and handed it to Trig.

"I'm going in alone," he said quietly.

"The hell you are, boss. What are we three here for? To take a nap? You're crazy. Excuse me, boss, but you're really nuts."

Jared smiled, then looked at Marcus, who was scanning the ceiling.

"Get it, Marcus?"

"Yep. How long?"

"I can only guess. Ten minutes."

"For what? For who?" Trig asked. "Marcus, our boss has flipped his switch. Talk to him. Oh, hell, forget that. It would take you ten years to string the words together. Finn, speak to this man. That's your sister in there."

"I follow orders," Finn said. "I'm not exactly a pro at this."

"Well, wonderful, just wonderful. Boss, listen to your old Trigger here. You can't go in there alone with no gun. Think of how upset your pretty Southern mama is going to be if the Mouse shoots her baby boy dead as a doornail. Mamas get upset about that stuff. Boss, think about Tabor."

"I am, Trig," Jared said quietly. "I'm definitely thinking about Tabor. Stay put. Marcus, ten minutes."

"Ten minutes for what?" Trig asked.

"Marcus will tell you."

"Good luck, Jared," Finn said. "My father trusted you, and so do Tabor and I. If this is how you think it should be done, then so be it."

Jared looked at Finn for a long moment, nodded, then opened the door and stepped out into the hall. As the door closed behind him with a soft swish, he started down the carpeted corridor.

He felt detached from himself, as though he were watching someone else counting off the steps that could very well be leading to death. He was vulnerable against the enemy waiting for him. Never during all his years as an agent had he walked into such a volatile situation with so little to defend himself with. He didn't need his little voice to tell him he was placing himself at great risk. He knew. But he had no choice, because Tabor needed him. It was because of him that her life was in jeopardy. It was his fault. His.

At the end of the corridor he stopped, flattened himself against the wall, and peered around the corner. There was no one down the hall standing guard outside his door.

Mason, he thought grimly, was a cocky little devil.

He strode down the hall, aware that the ten minutes he'd instructed Marcus to wait were ticking by. At his suite he knocked on the door with two staccato raps. The door was opened by a huge man in a dark suit who pointed a gun at Jared's chest. He waved the gun toward the interior of the room, and Jared stepped inside. The door was closed behind him, the click of the lock sounding like an explosion in the quiet room.

Jared's gaze quickly swept the area. Nick, Pico, and Joe were tied to chairs, adhesive tape covering their mouths. All three strained against their ropes when they saw Jared. Mason was standing next to the bookcase. Another man holding a gun was by his side.

And then he saw her. Tabor.

She was sitting in the center of the sofa, not tied or bound in any way. She looked at him, and as their gazes met, she smiled. To Jared it was the most beautiful smile he'd ever seen. His heart thundered as he read in her eyes her trust in him.

He didn't deserve that trust, he thought. Her life was in danger and it was his fault!

"Well, well," Mason said, "the great Jared Loring is not looking like his usual dapper self at the moment. It was a bit warm out at the cabin, wasn't it? I trust you found Finn O'Casey in good health?"

Tabor got to her feet. "You have Finn, Jared?"

Mason jerked his head at the man next to him, who moved to the end of the sofa.

"I have him, Tabor," Jared said. "He'd been drugged. It took about seven minutes to bring him around."

Tabor's mind raced. Seven minutes. Jared was trying to tell her that something was going to happen in about seven minutes.

"Oh, thank heavens," she said, her hands flying to her cheeks. "My brother is safe. Oh, that's wonderful." She spun around as though overcome with joy, stopping within a foot of the man standing by the end of the sofa.

"Enough festivities," Mason said, walking slowly forward. He halted a few feet in front of Jared. "You were good on this one, Loring, but I was better."

Jared nodded. "That's true, Mick. You won this one. I'd give you a high-five like they do on the street, but my hands are dirty. It was a tad grimy out at the cabin."

High-five, Tabor thought. Five minutes. Until what? She'd managed to move close to one of the men with a gun, but what should she do with him, to him, when the five minutes were up? Mickey Mason was right in front of Jared, and the other man was behind him, holding a gun pointed directly at the center of Jared's back. Oh, God, she was so frightened. Stay calm, she told herself. For Pete's sake, Tabor O'Casey, stay calm.

"So," Mason said, "let's conclude our business, shall we? I want the list, Loring."

"And then?"

"I'll walk out of here."

"Now, why don't I like the sound of that?"Jared said dryly. "I'm not hearing the right words, Mick. I'm not hearing you say that when you walk we'll all be left behind alive. It's been pointed out to me that my delicate Southern mama would get a case of the vapors if I were killed. A man has a responsibility to his mother, you know." He paused. "Well, maybe you don't know. Does a guy named Mickey the Mouse actually have a mother?"

Tabor gasped. Oh, Jared!

Mason's face flushed with anger. "Shut up, Loring. You're in no position to be mouthing off. I want that list—now! You seem to forget that your lady is one bullet away from being dead. She'll be first. I'll have her shot first, Loring, and you can watch. Damn you, I want that list, and I want it now."

Stall, Jared told himself. Two more minutes. What were the chances that Tabor, Nick, Pico, or Joe had picked up on his veiled message about time? Slim, very slim.

Suddenly Nick began to moan, his head rocking back and forth as he strained against the ropes binding him.

"He can't breathe," Jared said. All right, Capoletti! Nick had gotten the message. He was buying them time. "He has . . . sinus problems. He can't breathe well through his nose."

Despite his continuing performance, Nick managed to give Jared a dark glare.

"Mickey," Jared said, "the man is suffocating over

there." Come on, Marcus, do it. "No one should die that way. What in the hell am I supposed to tell *his* mother? Nick deserves a little dignity here." Oh, for crying out loud, this was really absurd. Well, desperate men did desperate things. Marcus . . . now!

From nearly invisible small spigots in the ceiling water gushed forth in heavy sprays. Water so cold it shocked the body, and so sudden it stunned the mind.

In a blur of motion Jared rammed one elbow into the man behind him. With a loud "oomph" the man bent over, dropping his gun as he staggered backward, clutching his stomach.

The man beside Tabor swung his gun around, but she grabbed his wrist with both hands and sank her teeth into the fleshy side of his hand, biting him with all she was worth. He yelped in pain and dropped his gun, trying to shake Tabor loose. She held on like a tenacious terrier refusing to give up a coveted bone.

"Good night, Mason," Jared said, and delivered a hard right cross to the round man's jaw. The Mouse crumpled to the floor. Jared grabbed the gun from the carpet and pointed it at the man Tabor was still tormenting. "Tabor, move away. Untie Nick if you can."

Tabor released her hold on the man. "Yuk. He tastes like garlic." She ran across the room to Nick.

Jared waved both of the big men onto the sofa, then opened the door. Water was pouring from the hall ceilings as well as continuing in Jared's suite. Everything and everyone was thoroughly soaked.

"Trig!" Jared yelled down the hall. "Marcus! Finn! Can you hear me? It's clear here. Come on."

Tabor managed to free Nick's hands. He tore the adhesive from his mouth, then set to work on the ropes at his feet. Tabor pulled the tape from Pico's and Joe's mouths, then Nick was up and helping her untie them. Trig, Finn, and Marcus came barreling down the hall and into the room.

"Tabor!" Finn shouted.

"Finn!" She ran to him, flinging herself into his arms and burying her face in the crook of his neck as he held her tightly to him. "Oh, Finn, Finn."

Jared uselessly wiped the water from his face as he stared at the brother and sister. He felt totally alone, separate and apart from all that was taking place around him.

"Nice work, boss," Trig said, pointing his gun at the two men on the sofa. "Wet, but nice. I couldn't believe it when Marcus told us to hold the flames from those lighters under the spigots in the ceiling."

"It sure turned them on," Jared said, "but how in the hell do you turn them off? Enough is enough."

"Oh." Marcus nodded and headed out the door.

"Up, Mason," Trig said to the now moaning man. "On the sofa. Line up like the three little pigs, Mickey Mouse."

Nick finished untying Pico and Joe, then crossed the room to Jared.

"Sinus trouble?" he said. "Was that as classy as you could get? I was stalling for you, and I get sinus trouble as my reward?" He glanced up at the spraying water. "What I'm going to get is pneumonia."

The water slowed, then stopped.

"Hey," Trig said, "I haven't shampooed my hair yet. Boss, this room is blitzed."

"Better it than us,"Jared said. "Let's take these guys downstairs. Tabor, get into some dry clothes. Finn, you'll fit in my stuff. Go in the closet in the bedroom and find something. You can change downstairs. This whole floor is drowned."

"What?" Nick yelled. "My suite is on the same sprinkler system? My stereo, my VCR, my African violet, can't swim. Everything will be ruined. I'm submitting a bill to you, Mouse Mason."

"Go to hell," Mason said sullenly.

"You really should work on your personality, Mouse," Nick said. "Sure can tell you're not Italian. You're not one bit charming."

"I'm really sorry, Mr. Loring," Pico said. "They came out of nowhere, had the drop on us before we knew what hit us."

"They won a round on me too, Pico," Jared said. "Don't worry about it. Trig, get this scum out of my living room. Pico, you and Joe help Trig take them down to the small office. Have Turtle get the word out that the Code Dark Blue alert is officially over. I'll be along in a minute."

"I'm going to go get dry clothes," Nick said. "I'm brave. I can handle seeing the watery destruction of all my worldly goods. So what if I cry like a baby? It won't mean a thing."

The group dispersed with Mason hurling threats at Jared. Jared waved a dismissing hand, paying no attention to the man's rantings and ravings. Tabor and Finn came out of the bedroom with dry clothes.

"All set?" Jared asked. "Good. Fine. You two go ahead. I'll grab some dry things and be there in a minute. I'll bring the list and contact the proper people to come pick it up, along with the Mouse and the Mouseketeers. Then I'm going to get some sleep, but not in this suite. Lord, what a mess."

Tabor walked slowly toward him, frowning when she stopped in front of him. "Jared? What's wrong?" She searched his face for some clue to what he was thinking.

"Nothing," he said, not meeting her gaze. "I'm cold, tired, even hungry. My suite is demolished. Listen, you were terrific in the crunch. When you bite someone, you don't mess around. You caught my message about the seven minutes too. Sharp, very sharp." He extended his hand, reaching beyond her. "Finn, you handled yourself well, right from the start. Cat would be proud of both of you."

Finn stepped forward and shook Jared's hand. "We're both very grateful for what you did for us."

Oh, dear, Tabor thought. Finn didn't know that Jared was adverse to expressions of gratitude. Jared was acting strangely as it was without Finn saying thank you.

"You're welcome," Jared said pleasantly. "No problem. Glad it all came together in our favor at the end. I'll meet up with you downstairs."

Oh, yes, there was definitely something wrong with Jared Loring, Tabor thought, staring at him again. The danger was over, Finn was free, the list would be taken care of, the nightmare with Mickey Mason was finished. Was everything over now? All that she had shared with Jared? Was this how quickly and easily he closed doors and moved on to whatever and whoever might be around the next corner?

She knew he didn't love her, but he hadn't even taken her into his arms, had barely looked at her. It was as though he were trying to get her and Finn out of there as quickly as possible.

No, now wait, Tabor told herself. Jared was cold, tired, and hungry. He needed warm clothes and hours of sleep, and he had yet to wrap things up with those waiting for him downstairs. She wasn't being fair. They'd talk later when there was no danger, fear, or exhaustion clouding their minds.

And then she'd see if she'd broken through Jared Loring's walls. She'd discover if she was going to have a chance to be his sunshine.

Eight

At midnight Jared threw back the blankets and swung his feet to the floor. He rested his elbows on his knees and dropped his head into his hands.

He was numb with fatigue, but sleep was an elusive treasure just out of his reach. Each time he closed his eyes, visions of Tabor crowded in on him, causing his body to ache with desire.

Tabor was in the room next to his, and it was so easy, and so tormenting, to picture her lying in bed, her hair spread out on the pillow, a soft smile on her lips as she lifted her arms to welcome him into her embrace, her body. Such sweet, beautiful lovemaking they would share. But . . .

"No," he said aloud.

He lay back down on his bed, lacing his fingers beneath his head and staring up into the darkness.

If he looked out the window, he would see Miracles on the other side of the street alive with bright lights, business as usual. Miracles was a gaming casino, not a hotel, and the second floor, now thoroughly soaked with water, was comprised of his, Nick's, and Tucker's suites, the office, and several smaller sleeping rooms for their special guests and family. Nick had booked rooms for Jared, Tabor, Finn, and himself at the hotel-casino across from Miracles.

Jared sighed. He had to get some sleep, he told himself. It had been a hell of a day, and there was more to come. Mouse and company were being held by the local police awaiting the arrival of federal agents. The list had also been turned over to local authorities, and all involved would be questioned the next day when the appropriate agents had gotten there.

More than that, he also had to hire crews to bring in equipment to dry out the soaked carpeting and furniture, determine what personal possessions were ruined and had to be replaced, and so on. Hell, what a mess . . . literally.

And sometime the next day, he thought, he was going to have to see and talk to Tabor. He'd done a dandy job of keeping out of her way after the fiasco in his living room. He'd left her in Finn and Nick's care, and managed to keep very busy speaking with the police, personally thanking each of his people involved in Code Dark Blue for a job well done, asking Turtle to make a list of companies who specialized in water damage.

He had not, Jared admitted, wanted to be alone with Tabor. He knew that his reluctance was born of his own inner confusion. A myriad of feelings were hammering at his mind, throwing at him a jumbled mass of unanswered questions. Emotions with no names created an ache within him beyond his physical desire for Tabor. At the center of the confusion was Tabor, beautiful Tabor, beckoning to him to come to her.

But he couldn't go to her, not yet, because the confusion was like an impassable jungle through which he couldn't find his way. He'd played over and over in his mind the fury and icy fear that had consumed him when he'd first realized Mickey Mason had outsmarted him and was holding Tabor captive. He'd felt so helpless, so inadequate. Stripped bare of his strength, cunning, and intelligence, he'd had to fight to regain his inner control.

When he'd walked alone down that hall to his suite where Mason held Tabor, a strange calmness had settled on him. He'd been prepared to die to obtain Tabor's safe release.

"Oh, Lord." Jared groaned and rolled over onto his stomach. He couldn't go on like this. This confusion was so foreign, so different from the tight control he kept over his mind and body. The answers lay with Tabor, and he would find them, sort through it all, understand it, then dismiss it as finished. No matter how strong the silken threads she'd woven around him were, he'd break them and be free. He wanted her out of his life, out of his brain—and he wanted to make love to her until the burning need within him was finally satisfied. "Hell. Sleep, Loring. Just shut up and sleep."

At last fatigue claimed him, and he slept, tossing and turning through the long, remaining hours of the night, dreaming of Tabor O'Casey.

Tabor awoke in the middle of the morning, wondered where on earth she was, then remembered so quickly that the fogginess of sleep was instantly whisked away.

She turned her head and saw that her arm was stretched across the empty bed. She'd been searching for Jared, she knew, just as she had in her dreams during the night.

Jared was avoiding her. She knew it, and so did Finn and Nick. She'd seen them exchanging looks and frowns every time Jared had given them instructions the afternoon before. Jared had spoken to the two men but had made no eye contact with Tabor, had not acknowledged her presence. And, Lord, that had hurt.

That Finn was aware of the tension between Tabor and Jared came as no surprise to her. She and Finn were so attuned to each other's moods and feelings, they'd long since given up any attempts to fool the other. Finn hadn't pressed her about Jared, but he would. He'd respected the fact that she was tired—so was he—and as Cat had always told them, "Things will be clearer in the bright light of morning."

Well, it was morning, Tabor thought dryly, and things weren't one bit clearer regarding Jared's sudden switch in attitude and behavior toward her. Unless . . . it was as clear as a bell, and she was refusing to face the fact that Jared had decided it was time to move on to greener pastures.

Well, baloney, she thought. She wasn't going to disappear quietly in the night, go back to California without a whisper of protest, and cry for five years straight. No, sir, after what she and Jared had intimately shared, plus what they'd been through because of Mickey Mason, he owed her an explanation for his chilling behavior toward her. He was going to have to look her square in the face, tell her it had been fun but was over, and *then* she'd go home to California and cry for five years straight. Jared Loring was going to talk to her, by gum.

A knock at the door startled her from her reverie, and she threw back the blankets and reached for her robe. She crossed the room as she slipped on the robe and tied the sash, then hesitated with her hand on the doorknob.

"Who is it?" she called.

"Finn."

Uh-oh, she thought. The inquisition regarding Miss Tabor O'Casey and Mr. Jared Loring was about to begin.

She opened the door. "Well, hi," she said, smiling brightly. "Oh! How nice. Breakfast. Push that cart right in here, brother dear. I'm starving." She stepped back as Finn entered with a cart laden with covered dishes, then shut the door. "You look so much better, Finn. Good as new. I hope your ribs aren't too sore. I hate the idea of those men hitting you. You do look super though. Let's bring those chairs over to the cart and see what you have here."

She slid a quick glance at Finn. He'd crossed his arms over his chest and was looking at her with a blank expression on his face. She put the chairs in place, sat down, and waited until he sat opposite her.

"Have you wound down yet," he asked pleasantly, beginning to remove the covers from the dishes, "or would you like to blither on for another ten minutes or so before we discuss you and Jared?"

"Darn it, Finn. Just once in your life couldn't you

be dense? Not have the foggiest notion about what's happening with me?"

"No."

She sighed. "I didn't think so. Did Nick say anything to you?"

"Not really. He mumbled something about Jared suddenly acting strangely around you and he'd like to shake some sense into him, but he didn't elaborate." Finn loaded food on his plate. "The tension was so thick between you and Jared yesterday, I could have cut it with a knife. He wasn't looking at you, you were looking at him like a very hurt and confused woman, and on it went. Eat some of this food, Tabor."

She spooned scrambled eggs onto her plate, filled her coffee cup, then nibbled on a piece of toast as she stared at the second button on Finn's shirt.

"Like that button?" Finn asked. "It's Jared's button, because this is Jared's shirt. You know Jared Loring, he saved our amateur-agent hides. Nice guy, that Jared, and every bit as tough and terrific as Cat had been telling us for years that he was. Do you like Jared's silver hair? It's classy. In fact, the man himself has class. Yeah, I think he's—"

"Would you stop it, Finn?"

"If you won't talk about him, then I will. Tabor, we're giving our statements to the feds today, then that's that. We can fly home, get on with our lives, put all this behind us. Is that what you want?"

Tabor's gaze flew up to collide with Finn's. "No. No, Finn, I'm not leaving here until Jared explains to me why he changed so suddenly. It will break my heart when he tells me, when he says the words out loud, but I have to hear it from him. I'm probably setting myself up to be hurt even more, but I have to do it this way." She sighed. "Oh, Finn, I love Jared so very much."

Finn nodded. "I thought you did. No, I knew you did. I could tell. I think Nick has figured that out too."

"Yes, he has. Nick said Jared loves me, but . . . Nick thinks that Jared doesn't understand his own feelings for me. Oh, I don't know."

"Tabor . . ."

"Finn, don't even hint that maybe I don't know my own feelings either. Don't say that the circumstances were far from ordinary, that I may have gratitude mixed up with love. I'm a woman who is in love for the first time in her life, and I know that love is real, the stuff of which forever is made."

"I believe you," Finn said. "You're in love with Jared Loring."

She blinked. "Oh." She nibbled on the toast again.

"Nick could be right, you know," Finn went on. "I can picture Jared being the kind of guy who might not realize he's fallen in love. He's lived a life that has called for total control. From what I hear, love can be a rather out-of-control emotion at times."

"That's for sure," Tabor said glumly. "It can be wonderful and awful in practically the same breath."

"Sounds like fun."

"It's really more wonderful than awful, except when the person you love isn't in love with you."

"You don't know that Jared doesn't love you."

"I don't know that he does either."

"And that," Finn said, leaning toward her, "is the bottom line. Find out exactly what Jared's feelings are toward you."

"Which could be tough to do, Finn O'Casey," she said, waggling the toast at him, "if the man in question doesn't even know what those feelings are."

Finn snatched the toast from her hand and took a big bite. She didn't notice.

"I want to be, I could be," she said softly, "Jared's sunshine."

Finn smiled warmly at her. "You do love him in all the right ways. I'll never forget how close to tears I was when Cat told us we were his sunshine. Jared would understand that, what it means, because he was, maybe still is in a way, a man of the night like our father was."

"Yes, I know Jared would understand. He asked me if you and I realized how important, how special it was that Cat had said that to us. Jared's sunshine is Miracles, but when I asked him if it was enough, he changed the subject."

"Interesting," Finn said. "Eat your eggs."

"I don't want them."

He reached across the table and took her plate. "Hate to waste these." He shoveled in a forkful, then refilled his coffee cup. "What do you have pending with your decorating business?"

"Nothing. I'd just finished that huge job for Mrs. Kenningston-Smith, and I was thinking of taking a short vacation. She was exhausting to work with because she changed her mind every other day."

"Well, I have to get back because I have a show scheduled. I've guaranteed the gallery a set number of paintings. But think about this, Tabor. The entire second floor of Miracles was soaked with water. They'll dry out what they can, but I'm sure some of that stuff is ruined. Certainly would be helpful if you volunteered your expertise in setting things to rights. After all, Jared did save our lives. It's the least you could do. You supervise the cleanup, bring in what new items are needed, be a Helpful Hannah. Strictly business."

"Strictly business," she said thoughtfully, tapping her fingertip against her chin. "Yes, because a man like Jared doesn't like to be pushed."

"Precisely."

"Why are you so smart concerning love?"

"Because, little sister, I'm *not* in love, which means my brain hasn't turned into oatmeal. I'm capable of viewing this situation objectively, with a great deal of intelligence."

"Well, la-di-da."

He laughed. "Do you want that glass of orange juice?"

When Finn had consumed every scrap of food, he announced that he was going to Miracles and would meet up with Tabor there. She said good-bye to him rather absently, sat deep in thought for ten minutes, then finally headed for the shower.

An hour later, dressed in white slacks and a blue and white striped blouse, her hair again in a single braid down her back, she entered the front door of Miracles Casino.

"Tabor," Nick called, hurrying toward her.

"Hi," she said, smiling at him.

"The feds are ready for you. They need to take your statement. They're using the small office down here."

"All right."

"How are you?" he asked, looking at her intently.

"Fine . . . I hope. Ask me again later, after I've seen Jared."

"Ah, the lady has a plan. Good for you. I didn't think you'd just leave without giving Jared Loring a run for his money."

"Have you seen him today?"

"Just for a minute. He didn't appear to be in a terrific mood. He had a don't-mess-with-me-I-eat-raw-meat expression on his face."

"Swell," she said gloomily.

"Go see the feds, then head for the second floor. Jared's up there trying to make order out of chaos. He had an outfit come in with fans and special drying vacuums, all that junk. It's a real mess."

"Dear, dear," Tabor said sweetly, "it sounds to me like Mr. Loring could use some professional decorating help. I'll speak with the agents, then toddle upstairs and see what assistance I can be." She started away. "See you later, Nick."

"Give him hell, Tabor," Nick called after her, a wide smile on his face.

It was more than an hour later before Tabor climbed the service stairs to the second floor and stepped into the hall. She could hear machines humming in the distance, and when she bent down and pressed her hand on the carpet, she found that it was dry.

She went in search of Jared, telling herself she wasn't a bit nervous, then admitting in the next breath that she was lying. What would he do, what would he say, when he saw her? Was there any hope at all that Jared did, indeed, love her, but simply didn't recognize the emotion for what it was? Or had he dismissed her and all they'd shared from his mind, the memories having never reached his heart?

She had to know. She had to discover the truth while, somehow, keeping her pride intact.

The door to Jared suite was open and she walked in. Jared's back was to her as he stood in front of the bookcase, his hands planted on his narrow hips. He was wearing faded jeans and a gray knit shirt with black trim around the collar and short sleeves.

Tabor drank in the sight of him, his broad shoulders, the enticing view of his buttocks, his long muscular legs, then her eyes moved up to linger on the silver glow of his thick hair. She gazed at him and remembered, and powerful desire curled deep within her. The machines hummed somewhere in the distance, but there in that room was only silence, and the echo in her ears of the wild beating of her heart.

Oh, how she loved Jared Loring!

"Jared?" she said softly.

He spun around. He took one step toward her, then stopped, shoving his hands into the back pockets of his jeans.

"Tabor," he said, nodding slightly. "You're looking well. Have you fully recovered from your ordeal?"

"Yes, I'm fine." He wasn't going to do it, she thought. He wasn't going to cross that room and take her in his arms. He'd started to come to her, then stopped, the bum. But why? What was he really thinking? "How are you?"

"Okay," he said. Actually, he was confused as hell and aching to kiss her, to feel her soft body nestled to him. "Have you given your statement to the agents?"

"Yes."

"Good." Dammit, he thought. Now she was free to

leave, go back to California, walk out of his life. But that's what he wanted, wasn't it? Yes, of course. But . . . hell, trying to think clearly was a hopeless, useless effort. "Finn seems fine. I saw him a little while ago."

"Yes, he's a bit sore but not too bad, considering. I saw you looking at the books. Are they ruined?"

"Some are. The way the water sprayed it hit a lot of them but didn't touch others."

She walked over to an end table and ran her hand across it. "Mahogany doesn't stand up well to moisture. All the furniture in here is mahogany. You can have it refinished, or replace it. The chairs and sofas will depend on the material used for the upholstery. The lamp shades will definitely have to be replaced. Each room on this floor will have to be examined to determine what can be saved and what can't." She turned to face him. "It will be time-consuming, but not terribly difficult if you know what you're doing."

"Which I don't," he said gruffly.

"I do."

"What?"

"Jared, I'm an interior decorator. I make my living knowing about fabrics, woods, draperies, knickknacks —everything in a home. You have a casino to run. Why don't you let me take over the project of restoring these rooms to order?"

"What about your own business in California?"

"I'm between jobs. Finn has to get back, but I don't have to leave right away. Would you like me to stay?"

Oh, Lord, yes, he thought. Stay. Stay here with him. No, maybe she shouldn't. How could he ever sort through his confusion about Tabor with her so close, with him burning with need for her? He didn't know what answer to give her. Where was his control? What was happening to him?

"Jared?"

"I—yes, that would be great, Tabor. Please do handle this mess."

"I'll have to make a lot of decisions regarding what can be salvaged and what has to be replaced. Do you trust me?"

He narrowed his eyes. Was she just talking about furniture now? he wondered. Trust her? With what? His jumbled mind and emotions? His mahogany tables? What?

"I'll leave the decisions regarding the restoration of this floor up to you," he said.

He wasn't giving an inch, she thought. His walls were higher than they'd ever been. So be it. She wasn't admitting defeat. Not yet.

"Well," she said, glancing around, "I'd better get to work. There's a lot to be done. Do you have a pad of paper and a pencil I can use?"

"Tabor . . ."

"I'd better check all the mattresses on the beds. Some may not be wet, depending on the weight of the bedspread and blankets. Then—"

"Tabor."

"Yes?" She looked at him.

"I know you don't understand why I'm—I'm behaving so differently around you. I owe you an explanation but . . ." He raked a hand through his hair. "I don't have one to give you right now."

She continued to gaze steadily at him.

"You're not going to make this easy for me, are you?" he said, frowning. "Aren't you going to ask why I can't explain myself at the moment?"

"No. I assume you're confused about some things, need some time to work it all through." Oh, please, Jared, be confused. That sounded so dumb, but if he *was* confused, there was a chance that as he unraveled his inner puzzle he'd discover that he loved her. Jared Loring being confused would be wonderful news for now.

He nodded. "I do have a lot on my mind. You know, this water disaster, dealing with the feds, my duties at the casino. I wouldn't go so far as to say I'm confused. I'm mentally busy." Oh, brother.

Ah, pride, Tabor thought, smiling inwardly. *That* she understood. Pride was keeping him from admitting his confusion. Pride was keeping her from flinging herself into his arms and declaring her love for him. Well, she was betting that Jared Loring *was* confused. If he knew it was over between them, he'd had the perfect opportunity to say so. Instead, she was to stay on and redecorate the damaged rooms. Time was on her side. Time and her love for Jared.

"My African violet croaked!" Nick yelled, striding into the room. "It was about to bloom, too, and it died a watery death. You can't even get the leaves wet on those things, let alone play Niagara Falls with them. I fed that plant, talked to it, named it Peaches."

Jared laughed. "Peaches?"

"Well, yeah. I'm crazy about peaches, so I named my plant after something I really like. It was a toss-up between calling it Peaches or Pasta. Anyway, it's beyond help. I can't even bear to look at it."

Jared shook his head. "Life is rough, isn't it? Madame Decorator, put one African violet at the very top of your list of things to be purchased. A despondent Italian is a pitiful sight to behold. We must bring the sparkle back to Mr. Capoletti's sad eyes."

"Yes, sir," Tabor said, smiling. "I'll see to it posthaste."

"Oh?" Nick said, all innocent. "Are you hanging around awhile, Tabor? Going to supervise fixing up the joint? Excuse me, that was not a respectful way to speak of this fine, soggy establishment. I'm just so depressed about Peaches that I'm not myself. Where was I? Oh, yeah, are you in charge of the spit and shine?"

"I am indeed," Tabor said. "It takes a trained eye to know what can be salvaged and what will have to be replaced. What I need first is a big pad of paper and a pencil, then I'm going on a tour of this entire floor."

"Ma'am," Nick said, crooking his arm, "it would be my honor and privilege to find you paper and pencil, and I will personally accompany you on your fact-finding tour."

She slipped her arm through his. "Why, thank you, Mr. Capoletti. You Italians are so . . ."

"Charming. I'm sure that's the word you were looking for. Shall we go?"

"Nick," Jared said, a slight edge to his voice, "isn't there something you're supposed to be doing for the casino?"

"Nope. Everything is under control. The floor is covered, all is well. I'm donating my free time to help restore this area to its former self because I'm such a nice person. I could be all in a snit, you know, because of my violet. I'm hiding my grief rather well, if I do say so myself."

"Hear, hear," Tabor said.

"Just put a cork in it, Nick," Jared said.

"Come along, Miss O'Casey," Nick said, nearly hauling Tabor off her feet as they left the room.

"Well, hell," Jared said to no one. "I could have taken her on the damn tour. I was going to get her the paper and pencil too. Oh, Loring, shut up." And another thing, he went on to himself. Tabor didn't seem exactly broken up over the fact that he hadn't touched or kissed or held her. He was aching for her, and she had stood there talking about wet mahogany.

He began to pace the floor.

And he'd insulted the socks off her. He'd said he was too busy mentally to figure out why he hadn't touched or kissed or held her, as though she were the last thing on his list of priorities. She hadn't even commented on that one. She'd just gazed politely at him, then the next thing he knew, she was sauntering out the door on Nick's arm.

What did a guy have to do to get some attention from Tabor O'Casey? Have his African violet named Peaches drown in the hundred-year flood? What about Jared Loring? Didn't she care? Hadn't the beautiful, incredible, special lovemaking they'd shared meant anything to her? It damn well better have.

Why did he feel like a five-year-old throwing a tantrum?

And why did he have the sneaky suspicion that he was even more confused than he had been an hour ago?

Nine

Jared scarcely saw Tabor during the next three days. When he did catch a glimpse of her, she either waved cheerfully as she hurried to heaven only knew where, or was deep in conversation with various workmen. He had given her a set of keys for all the rooms on the second floor, and he never quite knew where she was, or might turn up.

His mood was not wonderful, and he pictured himself once as a thermometer that had dipped to dark and gloomy and gotten stuck there. Jared Loring was not a happy man.

Finn had returned to California after thanking everyone involved in Code Dark Blue. He bid farewell to Jared with a firm handshake, a heartfelt expression of gratitude, and not one word about Tabor.

Finn O'Casey, Jared had later decided, should have pushed Jared for answers regarding his conduct in respect to Tabor. Finn had been remiss in his responsibilities as an older, protective brother. He should have determined just how Jared felt about

Tabor before blissfully flying home to Beverly Hills. He should have pressed, because maybe if he had, the insistence of an outside voice might have helped unscramble some of the confusing maze in Jared's mind. Coming to the conclusion that they just didn't make big brothers the way they used to, Jared continued on in his dark and gloomy mood.

On the fourth day he informed Nick that it would be best if they changed shifts for the time being. Jared would work days, Nick would cover the floor at night.

"It's fine with me," Nick said, "but why?"

"Because I should be available to answer any questions for Tabor about the repair work on the second floor. It's not fair to you, Nick, that it has fallen on your shoulders."

Nick shrugged those shoulders. "Tabor hasn't asked me anything. She obviously knows what she'd doing, and she simply does it. You should see the terrific African violet she got me. What a beauty. I named it Peaches in memory of Peaches. Anyway, go ahead and take over the floor right now. I'll catch a nap later, then be on tonight."

"Good," Jared said. "You don't happen to know where Tabor is, do you?"

"Tabor? Oh, well, she's spending the day at the shop that's oiling and whatever the mahogany furniture. She made it part of the deal that she could supervise the work."

Jared scowled. "She'll be gone all day?"

"Yep," Nick said, rocking back and forth on the balls of his feet. "Even said they'd be working late . . . very late. Since you and I have changed shifts,

I'll probably be the one to see her. Was there a message you wanted me to give her?"

"No," Jared said through clenched teeth, and stalked away.

Nick had the good sense not to laugh until Jared was well out of hearing range.

Late on the fifth day the furniture was returned, and Jared found a note on his bed from Tabor saying he was free to move back into his suite.

That night Jared spent several torturous hours in his bed trying to sleep. Memories of making love with Tabor in that bed kept him tossing and turning, aching for her. The visions in his mind became so real it was as though she were actually there, whispering his name as her hair and enticing aroma floated over him.

When he put his feet on the floor on the morning of the sixth day, his mood had dropped a notch below dark and gloomy. Standing in the shower with the water beating against his body, he came to a firm decision. He'd had enough. He'd made absolutely no progress in unscrambling the confusing emotions churning within him. Everything seemed to have gone on hold the day of the showdown with Mickey Mason. Being alone with his own thoughts, not really seeing Tabor, had accomplished nothing.

It was, he told himself, time to regroup, start over with a fresh plan. He would go to the source of his turmoil—Tabor O'Casey. She had the answers, the key to his regaining his sense of control. She was causing his dilemma and, therefore, was the means by which he would correct it.

It was time for action!

He would do whatever he had to do to obtain

inner peace. And Tabor? he wondered as he dried off. Hell, she didn't care. She hadn't made one attempt to seek him out, be where she knew he would be. There'd certainly been no thoughts of him causing *her* any distress as she'd scurried around decorating her little heart out.

Jared muttered a string of curses in several different languages as he dressed in jeans and a black T-shirt. Thug clothes, he thought. They fit his mood. There was anger edging in around the dark and gloomy, rip-roaring mad-as-hell anger.

He strode into the living room, picked up the phone, and punched in Turtle's number with such force, a sharp pain shot through his finger.

"Damn," he muttered, shaking his hand.

"No, it's Tuttle. The name is Mrs. Tuttle. I recognize that swearing. Hello, Jared sweets."

"Have Chuck cover the floor, Turtle," Jared said, peering at his throbbing finger.

"Oh? Something important on your agenda today?"

"That, Mrs. Turtle, is none of your business."

"Of course it is. I'm a nosy person, so everything is my business. That's how that works."

Jared rolled his eyes. "Just have Chuck cover the floor."

"You betcha." She paused. "She's doing a super job of fixing things up, isn't she?"

"Yes, she really knows—" Damn, he thought. "Who? Who is fixing what up?"

"Okay, Rhett, we'll play this your way. But in case you're wondering, I just had her paged because a big box of books was delivered. I'm having the books sent up to your suite because they're for you, and I plan to inform Miss Who that's where they are. She'll probably pop in there in a bit."

"Oh. Well, fine. Turtle, order me some breakfast, would you, please?"

"Order you some breakfast? You can't press a few numbers on the phone, open your mouth and say 'Eggs, toast, coffee'? Old age must be the pits. Personally, I wouldn't know. My body is sagging, but my mind is young."

"Forget it, just forget it. I'll order my own damn breakfast. I'll bite a bullet for the pain while I hit the numbers with my mangled finger. You're cold, Turtle, very cold."

"Oh, for Pete's sake, I'll get you some breakfast. Maybe it will improve your disposition. No, food won't do it. Food isn't what you need, Jared Loring."

"Meaning?"

"You figure it out. Good-bye. Some of us work around here." She hung up with a less than gentle touch.

"Fine, kill my ear," Jared mumbled, slamming down the receiver. "It'll match my finger."

There was a knock at the door, and he crossed the room. In the screen above the door he saw a man gripping a hand truck containing a large box.

He opened the door. "Books?"

"Yes, sir," the man said.

"Just put them over by the shelves."

"Yes, sir."

After the man left, Jared opened the box and began to stack the books on the floor. He knew they would be exactly the ones needed to replace those damaged by the water. There were empty places on the shelves where the ruined volumes had been removed, and Tabor would have made a careful and thorough list of what was to be purchased.

She was excellent at her job, he mused, looking at the title of a book. She probably had a thriving business in Beverly Hills. A business that was waiting for her to return, along with a brother who would welcome her home with open arms. And men? How many men were eager for Tabor to come back into the social scene over there? Dammit, how many?

"Jared?"

He stiffened, his back to her as he remained hunkered down by the books. He'd been so engrossed in his thoughts that he hadn't heard her unlock the door and enter the room. If he were still an agent, he thought, he would probably be a dead one.

"I'm sorry," Tabor said. "I didn't realize you were in here. Turtle said the books had been delivered, and I assumed you were on the casino floor since you've changed shifts with Nick. I'll come back later."

"No. Now is fine." Sneaky Turtle, he thought. She had known he was in the suite but hadn't told Tabor. "No problem," he said, planting his hands on his thighs and pushing himself to his feet. He took what he hoped was an undiscernible steadying breath, then slowly turned to look at Tabor.

His body's reaction to her was instantaneous. Heat poured through him. His heart thundered, and he felt as though he'd been punched in the solar plexus, causing the air to swoosh from his lungs.

Tabor, beautiful Tabor, was just a few feet from being drawn into his arms, held close to his aching body. She looked lovely in her mint-green sundress, her hair flowing down her back. She looked like a spring flower, a breath of fresh air.

She was . . . dear Lord, she was sunshine!

Tabor felt her knees tremble as she stared at Jared. He was magnificent, she thought. So big and strong, so masculine, and she loved him with all that she was. She'd kept out of his way these past days with the hope that he'd seek her out, say that he'd worked through his confusion and now knew that he loved her, wanted her with him for all time.

But he hadn't come to her. The distance that separated them now, she knew, was far greater than a dozen feet. And he hadn't moved an inch toward her to close the gap.

Still, she hadn't stepped forward either, she thought suddenly. There were walls between them, and not just Jared's. Hers were there as well. An invisible but solid fortress had been erected, and its name was pride.

Did she have the strength, she asked herself, the courage, to set her pride aside? To tell Jared of her love for him, meet him halfway across that room, her portion of the wall reduced to rubble? Wouldn't it take a stronger woman possessing a greater love to put her pride aside rather than to hide behind it? Wasn't Jared Loring worth the risk of stripping herself bare, standing emotionally vulnerable before him?

She lifted her chin and took one tentative step forward, then another. Her legs were unsteady as she moved slowly, her gaze never leaving Jared's, her eyes misting with tears. She stopped in the middle of the room.

"I'm meeting you halfway, Jared," she said, her voice quivering slightly. "I've come this far by destroying the wall of pride I'd constructed. It's gone. I have no defenses left. I'll say these words to you with nothing to protect me, but it doesn't matter because they must be said." She blinked back her tears. "Jared Loring, I love you with all my heart, my soul, my mind. You are the only man I've ever loved. You are my love, you are my life. And, Jared?" A sob caught in her throat. "You are my sunshine."

"Oh, God," Jared whispered. His hands curled into tight fists at his sides and he stared up at the ceiling for a long moment to gain some control over his raging, warring emotions. He looked at Tabor again. "Oh, Tabor."

The knifelike pain in Jared's gut slowly faded. The confusion that had held him in an iron grip lessened its hold slowly, and he finally saw what it was.

"Pride," he said, his voice raspy as he met her gaze. "Yes. Tabor, there was so much happening to me, and I didn't understand it. When we made love it was as though I had given a portion of my very being to you, passed it into your care. But I didn't feel empty for having done that. I was complete like never before, and that didn't make sense."

He shook his head. "I lost control of myself around you, continually. I have never known such fear as when I realized that Mason had you. It was my fault that he'd gotten to you—mine—and I felt hollow, empty, because Mickey Mason had the one person who made me whole. I knew when I walked down that hall to where you were that I would gladly die to assure your safety."

He swallowed heavily before attempting to go on. "I couldn't deal with it all, Tabor. The emotions were none I could name, none I'd felt before, and I was so damn confused, so angry with you for clouding my mind, stripping away the control I'd always felt I had to have. Pride, yes, my pride kept me from trying to explain to you what I was going through, tell you about the confusion that was like a knife twisting inside me."

He took one step forward.

"But no more," he said. "You're right about there being a wall still standing here between us. A wall I felt I had to have over the years to protect myself, my control, who I was. You shattered your wall with more courage than I've ever been witness to."

Another step.

"The emotions are becoming clear now, Tabor; the confusion is fading into oblivion. But unless I break down this wall I'll never reap the rewards of what is on the other side. You, your love, our future together. I don't need my almighty control if I have you. I can just be myself, Jared Loring, a man with strengths and weaknesses."

One more step.

"Tabor, I . . ." His voice was choked with emotion. "I . . . love you. That's what it all was, right from the beginning, and I didn't recognize what I'd never felt before. I love you, I want you, and I need you. Tabor, please, I need you to be my sunshine."

He took the final step that closed the distance between them, and the wall was dust, gone forever.

"Jared," Tabor said, tears spilling onto her cheeks.

She flung herself into his arms and was caught tightly against his chest. She buried her face in his neck as he bent his head to inhale the sweet fragrance of her silken hair. They clung to each other, holding fast, never again wanting to be separated from the one of their heart.

Jared lifted his head as Tabor raised hers, and

blue eyes and brown glistened with tears. Then he kissed her, sealing the bond, the commitment for a lifetime. The kiss deepened and their passions soared, the flame of desire burning away the lingering ghosts of the confusion, the hurt, the loneliness of the past days. Left in their wake were the warmth of love and the glow of sunshine.

"I love you, Tabor," Jared said, his mouth against hers.

"And I love you, Jared. I love you so very, very much."

"I want to make love to you. Now."

"Yes. I want y—"

A knock interrupted her.

"What—oh, hell," Jared muttered. "I had Turtle order me some breakfast." He circled her shoulders with his arm and they crossed the room. Jared glanced up at the screen, which was dark. "Great security system. The monitor is on the blink." He opened the door, then his mouth, but no words came out. Tabor's eyes widened.

"Excuse me, boss," Trig said, whipping a cart into the room. Tabor and Jared took a quick step out of the way. "Important business here."

The cart was set for two and included a bottle of champagne nestled in a silver bucket of crushed ice. Close on Trig's heels came Nick, carrying his precious African violet, which he set in the middle of the table with a great flourish.

"I'm lending Peaches to you for the occasion," he said, beaming. "What a romantic touch. Don't Italians just blow your mind?"

Spider, Pico, and Joe tromped into the room, and to Tabor and Jared's wide-eyed horror, combined their voices with Nick and Trig to sing at full volume the worst rendition of "You Are My Sunshine" ever to be executed. The five bowed deeply, spun on their heels, and headed for the door.

"Hold it," Jared yelled. "How did you know . . ."

"We didn't," Nick said, grinning. "We just hoped you'd come to your senses. You two are very stubborn people, you know. If you hadn't worked it out by now, this was to nudge you along. Guess you didn't need us, but it was a hell of a performance we gave you. Maybe we'll take it on the road. Enjoy."

And with that they were gone, closing the door behind them and leaving Tabor and Jared staring after them with rather bewildered expressions on their faces.

"They're crazy, all of them," Jared said finally.

"They're wonderful."

"Yes." He turned her to face him. "They're good people, good friends. They care about us, wanted to see us together and happy. Hell, *they* understood me before *I* understood me."

"That's all behind us now, Jared. The walls are gone. Pride will never stand in our way again."

He cradled her face in his hands. "Tabor O'Casey, will you marry me? Would you be willing to live here with me, share my life, be my wife? A casino is no place to raise kids, but we could get a house later and . . . I realize you have a business in Beverly Hills but . . . well, people decorate stuff here too, and . . . Tabor?"

"I was wondering if I was going to get a chance to answer. Yes, Jared, I'll marry you. Yes, yes, and yes," she said, smiling at him.

His mouth melted over hers as his hands sifted

through her luscious hair, then slid down to the gentle slope of her buttocks, nestling her against his hips, where his arousal announced his want of her.

Tabor sank her fingers into Jared's thick hair, pressing his lips harder onto hers. She savored the taste of him, and the feel of his manhood surging against her.

"Breakfast," he mumbled.

"Cold eggs are nice. Cold toast is nice. We can eat later."

He lifted his head and glanced at the cart. He laughed. "That Turtle doesn't miss a trick. There are little butane flames under those dishes. The food will stay warm for a long time." He swung Tabor up into his arms. "A very long time."

It was ecstasy. Their lovemaking held special meaning, an even greater depth than before as they envisioned the future they would share together. They had fought hard within themselves to win their private battles so they would be free to mesh, at last, into one total entity. They were the victors, and they cherished their love even more as it had not come easy, or without pain. It was theirs forever.

They touched, kissed, whispered endearments, and rose to heights of passion like none before. They gave and received all that they were, holding nothing back as they were hurled into a place of swirling colors and glorious sensations. They lost control and rejoiced in the freedom it brought them as they clung tightly to each other.

"I love you, Jared."

"Ah, Tabor."

Sated, content, they lay close, hands resting on glistening skin, waiting for heartbeats to quiet, breathing to gentle. They were in love. They were at peace.

When Jared's stomach rumbled, Tabor laughed, then wiggled free of his embrace and ran to the shower. He was right behind her.

Dressed again, they sat down to enjoy the breakfast which was still hot and delicious. Jared opened the champagne and they toasted their future, their friends and families, even lifted their glasses to Peaches the Violet.

"I must call Finn," Tabor said. "He'll be so happy for us, Jared. My father would be pleased too."

"I owe Cat O'Casey a great deal," Jared said. "If it weren't for him, I would never have met you."

The telephone rang at the same time there was a knock at the door.

"Brother," Jared said, getting to his feet. "We're not spending our honeymoon in this zoo, that's for sure. I'll get the phone, you get the door."

"Okay."

Jared crossed the room and picked up the phone as Tabor opened the door. Before Jared spoke into the receiver he glanced at the door, then did a double take as an extremely tall, very attractive brunette came into the room.

"Hello? Jared?" a voice yelled over the telephone.

"What? Yes." Jared stared at the woman, who smiled at him pleasantly. Tabor looked questioningly at the woman, at Jared, then at the woman again. "Who is this?" Jared said into the phone.

"Tucker. Jared, it's a boy. I had a boy. No, no, Alison had him, but I was right there the whole time. Lord, she was brave. I nearly passed out. Mercer—you know Mercer, the butler I inherited from my grandfather, Jeremy Daniel Boone? Anyway, Mercer was so shook up he drank eight cups of tea. Mercer hates tea. Jared, it's a boy! Seven pounds, six ounces."

Jared laughed. "Congratulations, Daddy. That's fantastic. I'll pass the word around here right away." He jerked in surprise as the brunette slid her arm across his shoulders and wiggled close to his side. He glanced at Tabor, who was watching with great interest, her eyebrows raised. "Tuck, could you hold on a minute? Don't hang up. I want to hear more about the Boone heir, but there's a situation here that needs my attention . . . fast."

"Yeah, sure, I'll wait," Tucker said.

Jared placed his hand over the mouthpiece. "Was there something you wanted?" he asked the woman, then frowned. "Bad choice of words. What can I do for you? Ah, hell, that wasn't any better."

"Try this," Tabor said calmly. "Lady, get your hands off that man, and use a total of three seconds to explain why you're here."

The woman quickly stepped away from Jared. "I'm a time-management consultant here on assignment to determine if Miracles is being run as efficiently as possible. Cutting wasted time is not only beneficial to profits, but to the employees themselves, as they're not as fatigued after their shift. I supply a valuable and much-needed service. My fee has been paid, and I can start work immediately."

Jared stared at her, then at the telephone. "Who paid your fee? No, I'll tell you. It was Tucker Boone."

"Why, yes, it was. He hired me in Houston and had me fly over. He implied that . . . well, that you and I just might hit it off on a personal basis, too, but . . ." She glanced at Tabor. "I can see this will be strictly business."

Jared laughed. "Tucker Boone," he yelled into the receiver, "you slimeball. Even with fatherhood pending you didn't forget that damn bet."

"Hey, she's sensational, Jared," Tucker said. "Super smart, super body. What more do you want?"

"Your head on a platter. Listen, what did you name that son of yours?"

"Ready? It's a great name. He's Jeremy Jared Nicholas Tucker Boone."

"Whew! That's a big handle for a little kid, but I'm honored to be included. Okay, I'll make the check out to him for one thousand dollars. I lost the bet, Boone, but you had nothing to do with it. I'll compromise by giving the money to the baby."

"You lost? You're in love?" Tucker whooped in delight. "I'll be damned. What do you mean, I had nothing to do with it? I sent her, didn't I? Boy, you're a fast worker, or she is, because I know she couldn't have been there more than—are you holding out on me, Loring?"

"I most certainly am, Boone. You can meet her at the wedding. In the meantime, die of curiosity, chum. Give my love to Alison and the baby. 'Bye, Tuck."

"Whoa! Wait! Jared!"

Jared hung up on a still hollering Tucker.

The woman shrugged. "Well, my fee is paid. Do you want me to go ahead with my study of Miracles?"

"Sure. Listen, do you like the strong, silent type?"

"I adore them."

"Then make sure you find a guy on the staff named Marcus."

"I'll make a point of it. 'Bye for now." She left the room.

"That was interesting," Tabor said after closing door.

"That was nuts, but I'll explain it all to you later." He opened his arms to her. "Come here, Mrs. Loring-to-be."

She moved eagerly into his embrace. "Tucker Boone has a new son?"

"Yes, and said son has a thousand bucks of my money. But, oh, Tabor, it's worth every penny. I've lost yet another bet with Tuck, and I'm so damn glad. I lost a bet but I won you, your love, our future together. i really came out the winner on this one."

"We have something else too, Jared," she said, smiling at him.

"Which is?"

"A lifetime of sunshine, my love."

THE EDITOR'S CORNER

We have some deliciously heartwarming and richly emotional LOVESWEPTs for you on our holiday menu next month.

Judy Gill plays Santa by giving us **HENNESSEY'S HEAVEN**, LOVESWEPT #294. Heroine Venny Mc-Clure and a tantalizing hunk named Hennessey have such a sizzling attraction for each other that mistletoe wouldn't be able to do its job around them . . . it would just shrivel under their combined heat. Venny has come to her family-owned island to retreat from the world, not to be captivated by the gloriously handsome and marvelously talented Hennessey. And he knows better than to rush this sweet-faced, sad-eyed woman, but her hungry looks make him too impetuous to hold back. When the world intrudes on their hideaway and the notoriety in her past causes grief, Venny determines to free Hennessey . . . only to discover she has wildly underestimated the power of the love this irresistible man has for her.

Two big presents of love are contained in one pretty package in **LATE NIGHT, RENDEZVOUS**, LOVE-SWEPT #295, by Margaret Malkind. You get not only the utterly delightful love story of Mia Taylor and Boyd Baxter but also that of their wonderfully liberated parents. When Boyd first confronts Mia at the library where she works, he almost forgets that his purpose is to enlist her help in getting her mother to cool his father's affections and late-blooming romanticism. She's scarcely able to believe his tales of her "wayward" mother . . . much less the effect he has on her. Soon, teaming up to restrain the older folks, they're taking lessons in love and laughter from them!

Michael Siran is the star twinkling on the top of the brilliantly spangled **CAPTAIN'S PARADISE**, LOVESWEPT #296, by Kay Hooper. Now that tough,

(continued)

fearless man of the sea gets his own true love to last a lifetime. When Robin Stuart is rescued by Michael from the ocean on a dark and dangerous night, she has no way of knowing that it isn't mere coincidence or great good luck that brought him to her aid. Indeed, they are both deeply and desperately involved with bringing the same ruthless man to justice. Before love can blossom for this winning couple, both must face their own demons and find the courage to love. Join Raven Long and friends for another spellbinding romantic adventure as "Hagan Strikes Again!"

You'll feel as though your stocking were stuffed with bonbons when you read **SWEET MISERY**, LOVESWEPT #297, by Charlotte Hughes. Roxie Norris was a minister's daughter—but certainly no saint! —and she was determined to win her independence from her family. Tyler Sheridan, a self-made man as successful as he was gorgeous, owed her father a big favor and promised to keep an eye on her all summer long. But Tyler hadn't counted on Roxie being a sexy, smart spitfire of a redhead who would turn him on his ear. She is forbidden fruit, yet Tyler yearns to teach her the pleasures of love. How can he fight his feelings for Roxie when she so obviously is recklessly, wildly attracted to him? The answer to that question is one sizzling love story!

You'll love to dig into **AT FIRST SIGHT**, LOVESWEPT #298, by Linda Cajio. Angelica Windsor was all fire and ice, a woman who had intrigued and annoyed Dan Roberts since the day they'd met. Conflict was their companion at every meeting, it seemed, especially during one tough business negotiation. When they take a break and find a baby abandoned in Dan's suite, these two sophisticates suddenly have to pull together to protect the helpless infant. Angelica finds that her inhibitions dissolve as her maternal qualities grow . . . and Dan is as enchanted with her as he is

(continued)

filled with anxious yearning to make the delightful new family arrangement last forever. A piece of holiday cake if there ever was one!

There's magic in this gift of love from Kathleen Creighton, **THE SORCERER'S KEEPER,** LOVESWEPT #299. Never has Kathleen written about two more winsome people than brilliant physicist Culley Ward and charming homemaker Elizabeth Resnick. When Culley finds Elizabeth and her angelic little daughter on his doorstep one moonlit night, he thinks he must be dreaming . . . but soon enough the delightful intruders have him wide awake! Elizabeth, hired by Culley's mother to look after him while she's on a cruise, turns out to be everything his heart desires; Culley soon is filling all the empty spaces in Elizabeth's heart. But healing the hurts in their pasts takes a bit of magic and a lot of passionate loving, as you'll discover in reading this wonderfully heartwarming and exciting romance.

It gives me a great deal of pleasure to wish you, for the sixth straight year, a holiday season filled with all the best things in life—peace, prosperity, and the love of family and friends.

Sincerely,

Carolyn Nichols

Carolyn Nichols
Editor
LOVESWEPT
Bantam Books
666 Fifth Avenue
New York. NY 10103